A Portrait of Hemingway as a Young Man
Romping Through Paris in the 1920s

By Jerome Tuccille
Award-winning, best-selling author of Gallo Be Thy Name
and other books

Blue Mustang Press
Boston, Massachusetts

ISBN: 978-1-935199-01-4
PUBLISHED BY BLUE MUSTANG PRESS
www.bluemustangpress.com
Mansfield, Massachusetts

Printed in the United States of America

A Portrait of Hemingway as a Young Man

Romping Through Paris in the 1920s

"Do not worry. You have always written before and you will write now. All you have to do is write one true sentence. Write the truest sentence that you know."

Ernest Hemingway in *A Moveable Feast*

Author's Note

This book is part satire, part homage to the men and women whom many regard as perhaps the greatest literary generation in modern times. Like other writers of my generation, and the generation that came before me, I grew up in the shadows of Ernest Hemingway, F. Scott Fitzgerald, Thomas Wolfe, William Faulkner, and other great writers of the early twentieth century.

I did not want to be *like* Ernest Hemingway; I wanted to *be* him. And so did Norman Mailer, George Plimpton, and a few others who sprung from the generation between Hemingway's and mine. Norman Mailer acknowledged Hemingway as "the heavyweight champion" of American writers. Then, in a singular display of self-promotion, Mailer declared that he was "the new heavyweight champion" after Hemingway splattered his brain on the ceiling of his house in Idaho with a well-placed shotgun blast.

I have written this book with my tongue firmly planted in my cheek, but also with great respect and admiration for Hemingway, Fitzgerald, Gertrude Stein, James Joyce, Ford Madox Ford, Morley Callaghan, and other truly fine writers of perhaps the most glamorous era in twentieth-century literature. I have wanted to write this book for some time now for therapeutic as well as literary reasons.

And now it is done. I have purged myself of the demons of the past—the giants who have haunted me all my adult life. God bless writers all over the world. And God bless writers who bend themselves to their craft because to spend their lives doing anything else is nothing less than the height of folly and self-destruction.

PART ONE

FOR WHOM THE SUN RISES

Chapter One

You know how it was in Paris in the 1920s. So many great writers lived there then. They blew in like the weather at one time or another through most of the decade. Ernest Hemingway, F. Scott Fitzgerald, James Joyce, Ford Madox Ford, Morley Callaghan, Robert McAlmon, and others of their ilk. Yes, they blew in with the weather, the good weather and the bad weather. It is not clear whether the bad weather blew in the good writers or the bad writers, or whether the good writers blew in with the good weather that always came later.

Gertrude Stein held court regularly at her weekly soirees. Established writers visiting Paris and those who aspired to immortality converged at Stein's apartment at 27 rue de Fleurus to pay homage to the great lady, the literary godmother of Paris. Miraculously, she had achieved that exalted status with self-published books that regular publishers refused to bring out because of her impenetrable writing style.

Gertrude and her brother Leo had moved into the large, gray, stone building just off the Luxembourg Garden long before the Hemingways arrived in 1921. Gertrude and Leo adorned the whitewashed walls of one of their rooms with masterpieces from many of the major painters of the era. Paintings by Renoir, Gauguin, Matisse, Picasso, Cezanne, Vallatton—including a portrait he did of Gertrude—El Greco, and others soared from floor to ceiling in tightly spaced columns. When Gertrude and Leo had a nasty spat in 1907, Leo moved out and Gertrude's lover, Alice B. Toklas, moved in. Ernest and his wife Hadley first came to visit early one evening in 1922, after Sherwood Anderson sent Gertrude a letter introducing Ernest as perhaps the most gifted among the latest crop of young American writers.

When Ernest and Hadley were admitted into Gertrude's inner

sanctum, *the maharani of letters* was sitting in a corner chair dressed in a long brown robe, her thick dark hair piled high on her head. She assigned Alice the task of keeping Hadley entertained while she took Ernest's measure. On a subsequent visit, Gertrude taught Ernest how to cut Hadley's hair real short, the way he liked it on her, in a sort of butch bob brushed forward Julius Caesar-style that Gertrude sometimes adopted for herself.

A lot of university professors and Hemingway scholars interpreted that to mean that Ernest was sexually conflicted and didn't know whether he preferred to fuck men or women. Then again, perhaps he just liked to fuck older women with short hair. Based on the evidence, he enjoyed sex with all kinds of women to the consternation of his wives and some professors.

* * *

Gertrude Stein was not pretty, quite the opposite in fact. Short, stout, severe of countenance, she had large breasts and sturdy legs. No, she was anything but pretty. But Ernest wanted to fuck her anyway. She reminded him of his mother Grace back in Chicago. "Her breasts weigh about ten pounds each," he said to Hadley.

"I always wanted to fuck her and she knew it and it was a good healthy feeling and made more sense than some of the talk," Ernest confided to one of Stein's biographers when he was drunk. The talk Ernest referred to was Gertrude's theory about homosexuality, which she said was good for women but not for men for reasons that never made all that much sense to Ernest.

For her part, Gertrude enjoyed the occasional dalliance with a man. At different times she had had intimate relationships with Pablo Picasso, Sherwood Anderson, and other men even when she was living with Alice. Alice knew about Gertrude's heterosexual flings, but she never considered them a threat to her own relationship with the quirky but influential writer.

But Alice *was* jealous of Ernest's presence at the soirees and his flirtatious exchanges with Gertrude. He was a big, burly guy who stood an inch over six feet tall, a natural two hundred-pounder who kept himself in good physical trim, but his dark liquid eyes harbored a sensitivity that belied his macho exterior. Alice was struck by the notion that there was something of a disturbing sexual undertone between Gertrude and Ernest. She was old enough to be his mother and had a decidedly masculine nature. He was the young courtier seeking her literary approval, a boy-man only twenty-three years old in need of a mother-substitute, and Alice was concerned about the oedipal aspects of their budding friendship. After all, Hadley was eight years older than Ernest, proof positive that Ernest liked to fuck older women.

Alice B. Toklas wrote that Ernest had "dark, luminous eyes," a "flashing smile," and long dark hair that "made him look like an Italian." His trimmed dark mustache completed the image. She feared him and, consequently, ended up hating him and was determined to separate him from Gertrude's circle of admirers and sycophants as soon as possible.

Ernest got what he wanted from Gertrude without actually having to fuck her. She opened doors for him to all the important literary salons of Paris, even though she told him that the content of one of his stories, "Up in Michigan," was *inaccrochable*, like a painting that cannot be hung and was therefore not marketable, a story that was essentially not publishable—a judgment that more aptly applied to her own literary efforts.

*   *   *

When Ernest was not at Gertrude's sizing up his competition, taking the measure of those who were not worth worrying about and those whom he regarded as serious threats—those whom he would have to challenge to a boxing match and prove his superiority later—he could usually be found at one of the myriad cafés on the Left Bank, writing his stories, having a drink, and observing all the drunks.

The Café des Amateurs was crowded, and the windows fogged over with heat and smoke and bad breath. The café was a truly evil café, crowded with all the winos from the quarter. Ernest would rather have gone elsewhere because he couldn't abide the sour smell of men and women who were drunk all the time, at least whenever they could afford it, drunk mostly on wine they bought by the half-liter or liter, but never by the pint or quart since only Americans or Brits measured their booze in ounces.

The women were known as female rummies.

But the drinks were cheap at the Café des Amateurs, so Ernest put up with the foul smells and wrote his stories, sipping a milky green absinthe or a St. James rum, and staring out the window from time to time to watch the wind and rain strip the leaves from the trees and blow them into the puddles on the rue Mouffetard.

One of the writers whom Ernest met early on, a man who would remain a friend for a few years afterward despite Ernest's shabby treatment of him, was Lewis Galantiere who was several years older than Ernest. Galantiere was an American journalist from Chicago, a playwright, and translator of French literature into English and American literature into French. He worked for the International Chamber of Commerce in Paris for most of the 1920s and later became president of the American branch of P.E.N.

Galantiere met Ernest and Hadley for dinner at the Restaurant Michaud, an upscale establishment where the food was good but fairly expensive. Ernest and Hadley, who lived on a tight budget, were relieved when Galantiere told them the meal was on him. The three of them got along fine until about midway through the evening, when Ernest noticed that Hadley was more than a little taken in by Galantiere's sophisticated taste and witty charm. At that point, Ernest asked Galantiere if he knew anything about boxing. Galantiere admitted to a passing familiarity with the sport, but little more. Ernest, fully fueled by now with the lion's share of the copious wine supply, began to terrorize his host with a story about how he had beaten up a professional fighter from Salt Lake City on his way across the Atlantic during a three-round exhibition match.

Would Galantiere care to join him for a friendly postprandial match back at his hotel? Ernest asked. Galantiere's eyes bulged with fear, but Ernest refused to take no for an answer. In their room at the Jacob Hotel where Ernest and Hadley were staying temporarily, Ernest stripped to the waist and helped his new buddy—the gentleman who had just wined and dined them royally—lace up a pair of boxing gloves that Ernest had brought over in his steamer trunk. There was no way out of it now. Galantiere's protests that he didn't like to hit other people, any more than he liked to be hit, fell on deaf ears. Ernest laced on his own gloves with Hadley's help, handed his stop watch to her, and told her to count out three-minute rounds.

Ernest and Lewis circled each other warily during the first round, with neither man throwing a serious punch. Morley Callaghan, a Canadian writer whom Ernest had met when they both worked as reporters for the Toronto *Daily Star*, described Ernest as a "rough, tough" piece of work who was most dangerous during the first couple of minutes of a fight. Ernest, he said, was capable of knocking a man out with a powerful overhand right if he landed it cleanly. But he was more of a brawler than a boxer, a man who depended on brute strength rather than boxing finesse.

Hadley gave the sign that the first round was over, and Lewis was relieved to have survived it with his jaw intact. He lowered his guard and put on his eyeglasses, smiling, indicating that the boxing match was over as far as he was concerned. Ernest shadow-boxed beside him, waiting for the next round to begin. When Hadley started the second round, Ernest simply walked up to Lewis, sucker-punched him in the face, and broke his glasses. Ernest was all apologies after that, helping his stunned dinner companion regain his composure, draping his brawny arm across Lewis's shoulder, expressing sympathy, telling Lewis he was a real sport. *Now* the fight was over. Ernest had demonstrated his superiority over his new friend. He had shown himself to be the dominant male in Hadley's eyes, the alpha male in the room, the champ.

In the Bronx where I grew up, Ernest would have been known as a real prick—a fun guy to have a drink with, a good guy to have on your side if a brawl broke out, but someone to keep your eye on as the evening progressed because you never knew when he might turn on you.

Chapter Two

Lewis was willing to overlook the incident and chalked it up to too much wine. He even went so far as to help Ernest and Hadley find an apartment in a neighborhood they could afford. Ernest and Hadley set up housekeeping in a two-room flat on the fourth floor of an old building at 74 rue du Cardinal Lemoine, with the toilet out in the hallway. Hadley had an income of three thousand dollars a year from a trust fund, and Ernest earned about half that amount as a free-lance journalist—a decent enough income at the time—so they were not exactly poverty-stricken. But Ernest wanted to use a lot of that money to travel around Europe, so he was willing to scrimp on their living arrangements since they did not yet have any children to worry about.

Ernest and Lewis remained on good terms until Ernest took the opportunity to attack him in print. Knowing that Lewis occasionally wrote book reviews under the pen name Lewis Gay, Ernest denounced Mr. Gay as essentially an effete snob in his column for Ford's *The Transatlantic Review.* Ernest then boasted to Ezra Pound that he had proven "in a squib for Ford that Galantiere is a little Jewish boy and a fool."

For all that, even Ernest's critics denied that he was anti-Semitic. Harold Loeb, a Jewish writer whom Ernest excoriated in his first novel, said he didn't believe that Ernest was an anti-Semite. Talk about "kike lawyers" and such was in the air then like talk about "wops" and other pejoratives, and Ernest slung them around along with the other slang of the day. He had his other measures for judging people, but ethnicity was not among them.

The bad weather was still blowing in lots of other writers, some of whom Ernest didn't want to see, so he suggested that they leave town and go to a place where he and Hadley could enjoy the snow. He knew about a chalet below Les Avants where they could read their books, snuggle together in bed, and take long walks in the snow and listen to it creaking under their boots.

"I think it would be wonderful, Tatie," said Hadley when he told her about it. "When should we leave?"

"Whenever you want."

"Oh, I want to right away. Didn't you know?"

The weather was fine and clear when they got there. They read their books and snuggled. Some Hemingway scholars envisioned them switching roles in their lovemaking, he on top, she on top, she straddling him with her short butch bob, taking turns being the aggressor, just like the couple in Ernest's posthumous novel *The Garden of Eden*. All in all, it was a glorious vacation with cold, clear, sunny days, and lots of reading, hiking, and lovemaking.

The weather had changed for the better when they returned to Paris. It was clear and cold and lovely. Ernest had trouble getting back into the writing until he told himself that all he had to do was write one true sentence, the truest sentence that he knew, and the rest would follow. "You have always written before and you will write now," he counseled himself. Ernest and Hadley went off to visit Gertrude and Alice to tell them of their trip to the mountains and his progress with his writing.

When they got there, Gertrude was full of sage advice about writing, clothes, paintings, and life in general. "You can either buy clothes or buy pictures," she told him. "It's that simple. No one who is not very rich can do both." Ernest discovered that Gertrude had become increasingly frustrated because she was having a difficult time finding a publisher for her work.

"I want to be published in the *Atlantic Monthly* or *The Saturday Evening Post*," she said. "You're not good enough yet to be published there, but you might be someday as long as you remember not to write stories that are *inaccrochable*."

The more Ernest got to know Gertrude, the more he realized that her main problem was her lack of discipline. In his estimation, she had written some truly fine experimental pieces, but much of her work was unintelligible because she hated to revise it. She thought everyone should recognize her for the genius that she was and let it go at that. One of the writers who blew in with the weather a bit later, Ernest's old journalist buddy from Toronto Morley Callaghan, was perhaps Gertrude's harshest critic. He thought she was a complete fraud who wrote the way she did, obscure incomprehensible gibberish in his view, because she had nothing important to say.

Some of the writers whom Ernest would rather have avoided also popped in on Gertrude and Alice periodically. Among them was writer and publisher Ford Madox Ford. Ford had incited Ernest's wrath by publishing some of Ernest's early stories in his literary magazine *The Transatlantic Review*. There were essentially two ways to get on Ernest's ugly side. The first was by crossing him in some way, and the second was by helping him or doing him a favor. Ernest hated to be obligated to anyone, to be reminded that he was not always the heavyweight champion of American writers who needed support in the early years. If you supported Ernest too ardently, you ran the risk of him challenging you to a boxing match. But Ernest *did* like to help other writers, particularly those whom he didn't think were as good as he was. He actually persuaded Ford to publish Gertrude's interminable, uneven, repetitious novel *The Making of Americans* serially in *The Transatlantic Review*, figuring that Ford's magazine would go bankrupt before he got to the last installment.

* * *

Gertrude continued to educate Ernest on the finer points of sex every opportunity she had. He seemed particularly stubborn on the subject of homosexuality. Ernest told Gertrude that he had certain prejudices against homosexuality because he knew its more "primitive aspects."

"It was why you carried a knife and would use it when you were in the company of tramps when you were a boy," he said. "When you were a boy and moved in the company of men, you had to be prepared to kill a man, know how to do it and really know that you would do it in order not to be interfered with. If you knew you would kill, other people sensed it very quickly and you were let alone."

Gertrude was properly horrified. "Yes, yes, Hemingway, but you were living in a milieu of criminals and perverts."

Ernest mentioned the name of an older writer she knew and asked Gertrude what she thought about him.

"No. He's vicious," she said. "He's a corrupter and he's truly vicious."

"But he's supposed to be a good writer."

"He's not. He's just a showman and he corrupts for the pleasure of corruption."

Then Gertrude reiterated her opinion of male versus female homosexuality, which Ernest never ceased to wonder about. "You've met known criminals and sick people and vicious people," she explained. "The main thing is that the act male homosexuals commit is repugnant and ugly and afterwards they are disgusted with themselves. They drink and take drugs to palliate this, but they are disgusted with the act and always changing partners and cannot be really happy." It was different with women, she said, whose acts were not repulsive so afterwards they could lead happy lives together.

Ernest mentioned the name of a female homosexual they knew who did not appear to be happy at all.

"She's vicious," Gertrude said. "She corrupts people."

It was not clear who was baiting whom in this exchange. Did Ernest really believe it was just fine to carry a knife so that you were prepared to kill the first man who put his hand on your testicles? Did Gertrude truly believe that what women did was wonderful but what men did was not? How about heterosexual sodomy, which some Catholic countries tolerated as a form of birth control? Was that equally disgusting? Was anal intercourse acceptable in that case while the use of a condom in vaginal intercourse was unacceptable because it subverted God's desire to populate the earth with more Catholics whether their parents could afford to feed them or not?

Oh, it was all so confusing! Ernest ended that conversation with a smile on his face, saying he understood. Gertrude glared at him, making it quite clear that she was sure he did *not* understand.

When Gertrude was not educating Ernest about sex, she was expounding on the books he should be reading. Ernest told her he was reading Aldous Huxley.

"Huxley is a dead man," said Gertrude. "Why do you want to read a dead man? Can't you see he is dead? You should only read what is truly good or is frankly bad."

"I've been reading truly good books all winter and all last winter and I'll read them next winter, and I don't like frankly bad books."

"Why do you read this trash?" she asked. "It is inflated trash, Hemingway. By a dead man. Who else do you read now?"

"D. H. Lawrence. He wrote some very good short stories."

"I tried to read his novels," said Gertrude. "He's impossible. He's pathetic and preposterous. He writes like a sick man."

Ernest had never heard Gertrude speak well of any writer who had not written favorably about her own work, except for Ronald Firbank and F. Scott Fitzgerald for whom she made allowances for reasons known only to her. She particularly loathed James Joyce, whose prose was even more incomprehensible than hers—although Ernest admired him. You could not even mention Joyce's name in Gertrude's presence. If you brought his name up twice, she would never invite you back.

Alice B. Toklas glowered at both of them. "Ernest has got to go," she seemed to be saying to herself. This was a dangerous relationship that was brewing between him and Gertrude. He seemed to be fascinated with her ten-pound breasts. And besides, she was getting tired of entertaining Hadley while Ernest and Gertrude discussed all these controversial issues. Hadley was sweet. She was truly beautiful with her short reddish blonde hair, those sparkling ice-blue eyes, that perfectly straight Grecian nose, that wholesome Midwestern glow of hers, those full pink lips. But there was something banal about her as well. She clearly worshiped her younger husband and doted on every word he uttered. But she was guarded about expressing an original thought of her own, afraid that she might say something that Ernest disapproved of.

Ernest would have to go sooner or later.

Chapter Three

Hadley was pregnant. Perhaps it happened on their short vacation near Les Avants. Could the conception have occurred while she was on top, he was on top? Would the position have anything to do with the sex of the child? Only the psychobabblers knew about that. For the rest of us, there was simply no way to know.

They returned to Toronto so Ernest could earn some money covering stories for the *Star*. Ernest's reputation as an up-and-coming fiction writer who lived on the Left Bank in Paris and associated with the likes of James Joyce, Gertrude Stein, and other well-known writers had preceded him across the Atlantic. Already he had achieved celebrity status in the newsroom and was treated to a hero's welcome, one of their own who had escaped to a more glamorous world and appeared to be destined for recognition and fame. Most of the reporters had met Hadley before she and Ernest had left for Paris and were totally enamored of her.

Greg Clark, one of the *Star* reporters, described Hadley as "gorgeous. I fell head over heels for Hadley. Gorgeous red hair and gorgeous on the piano."

"Hemingway was a great romantic figure, and Hadley fit into that," said Morley Callaghan. "He was very proud of her, and he talked about her a lot." Morley said that Ernest had a gift for making people want to talk about him, to make up stories about him that got embellished over time, turning him into someone larger than life before he actually was.

Of course Ernest was not exactly reticent about image-building. No one was better than he when it came to self-promotion and myth-making. While Hadley was entertaining Ernest's colleagues on the piano, Ernest was not beyond removing the Italian officer's cape that he had brought home with him from World War I, where he had served as an ambulance driver, and demonstrating some of the bullfighting moves he had seen in Madrid. With *chutzpa* like that, who needed a press agent?

But Ernest hated every minute of it and knew he had made the biggest mistake of his life in leaving Paris. With Ernest away on a writing assignment in New York City to cover the arrival of British statesman David Lloyd George, Hadley gave birth to a boy at two o'clock in the morning on October 10, 1923, and they named the boy John Hadley Nicanor Hemingway. Their pet name for him was Bumby. Hadley said that Ernest was furious that he had to be away. He hated being a journalist at the beck and call of his tyrannical editor in Toronto and couldn't wait to have a great success with a novel so that he could come and go when and where he pleased.

"He left practically in tears," said Hadley, "because he sensed that the birth was going to happen while he was away. Of course I missed Ernest horribly. He should have been right there with me, suffering. I was laid out on a table working away, pushing."

Ernest resigned soon after he returned to Toronto and made arrangements to return to the literary scene in Paris, where he knew he belonged. The couple needed a new apartment, something a bit larger in a better neighborhood with the toilet inside the flat and not as many rummies and prostitutes in the street outside. They found what they were looking for at 113 rue Notre-Dame-de Champs, a roomier flat over a sawmill near the Closerie des Lilas, a café where Ernest liked to write his stories, have a drink, and observe the people passing by. But while the new flat was larger than their earlier one, it had no gas or electricity. When Ernest finished writing for the morning, he would go over to visit Gertrude by himself since Hadley was occupied with her baby.

"Did you have a good talk with Gertrude?" Hadley asked when he returned to their flat.

"Yes, but she does talk a lot of rot sometimes," he said.

"I never hear her," said Hadley. "I'm a wife. It's her friend that talks to me."

* * *

After Ernest returned to Paris, he was more determined than ever to push ahead with a novel and liberate himself from the drudgery of writing journalism on demand, writing stories that other people ordered him to write instead of those he wanted to write. But he did acknowledge his debt to journalism. Covering stories for a major newspaper taught him how to write short declarative sentences, to hook the reader from the start with an enticing lead paragraph, getting to the heart of the story, knowing what to put in and what to leave out.

Ernest was happy to be in the railroad flat above the sawmill that had a small bedroom between the kitchen and the living room. Ernest described it as "very fine" with a great view. "All the trees are changing color and beyond the ravine you can see the open country."

Both parents were taken with their newborn child. In a letter to a friend, Hadley described "his big eyes, still blue, set wide apart … and the most exquisite little ears set well back and close to his head—has lots of dark brown hair too and a large Hemingway nose—stunning build—and healthy … "

Ernest was also taken with the boy. "The baby nurses very hard but cannot find the place at first," he wrote. "Then he makes a noise like a little baby pig. He is very small and has a beautiful body. Hadley let me lift up his clothes to look at his legs and back. He is very perfect and his body is very beautiful." But it was not too long before he was complaining about the baby's demands on his time; he *was* a writer after all, first and foremost.

"All the gang went deer hunting last Friday but me," he wrote to his father. "The baby has taken to squalling and is a fine nuisance. I suppose he will yell his head off for the next two or three years. It seems his only form of entertainment. No one gets as much pleasure out of it as he does."

On March 16, 1924, Ernest and Hadley made arrangements to have their son christened in an Anglican church where James Joyce's son Georgio sang in the choir. For godparents they chose an unlikely trio: Gertrude and Alice as joint godmothers, and Ernest's war buddy from World War I, a Northumberland Fusilier named "Chink" Dorman-Smith, as godfather. So it came to pass that two Jewish lesbians and an Irish Catholic professional soldier swore a vow to help Bumby renounce the devil and all his evil works throughout his life.

* * *

Sylvia Beach had short hair, but there was no indication that Ernest wanted to fuck her. She had a vivacious sculptured face, sparkling brown eyes, and wavy brown hair that she brushed back away from her forehead rather than combing it forward Julius Caesar-style like Gertrude would do later. She also had firm, well-tapered legs that caught Ernest's attention immediately.

She was the proprietor of Shakespeare and Company, a library and bookstore at 12 rue de l'Odean. She took a liking to Ernest and lent him books that he said he would pay for later, when he made more money from his writing. She lent him novels by Turgenev, Dostoyevsky, and D. H. Lawrence. Even though Gertrude thought Lawrence's stuff was *inaccrochable*, Ernest insisted on reading more of him.

"I'll be back to pay," said Ernest.

"You pay whenever it's convenient," she said.

"When does Joyce come in?" he asked.

"If he comes in, it's usually very late in the afternoon. Haven't you ever seen him?"

"We've seen him at Michaud's eating with his family. But it's not polite to look at people when they are eating, and Michaud's is expensive."

To make their money stretch further, Ernest told Hadley that it would be a fine thing to bet on horses if you had a good feeling about which ones were likely to win. Ernest, knowing that many of the European steeplechase races were fixed, had a tip that they should put their money on a long shot, a horse that paid big odds so they could leverage their money.

"Do we have enough money to really bet, Tatie?" Hadley asked.

"No. We'll just figure to spend what we take. Is there something else you'd rather spend it for?"

"Well."

"It's been terribly hard and I've been tight and mean about money."

No, but…" she said.

Mark Twain had said it best a few decades earlier: "There are two times in a man's life when he should gamble, when he can't afford it and when he can." He might have added a third time: when you know which horse is supposed to win.

Case closed. Hadley understood the wisdom in that as well as Ernest did. "I think we ought to go," she said. We'll take a lunch and some wine. I'll make good sandwiches."

They packed up their lunch and went off to the track with Bumby in tow. The train from the Gare du Nord took them through the sleaziest part of town, even shabbier than the neighborhood they lived in before moving to the flat above the sawmill. When they got to the track, Ernest uncorked the wine while Hadley unpacked the sandwiches. Ernest remembered an earlier time at Auteuil when Hadley had bet on a horse named Chevre d'Or, a hundred-and-twenty-to-one shot who was leading by twenty lengths until he tripped on the final hurdle and dashed their dream of living off their winnings for the next six months.

Today would be different. Hadley lay back on Ernest's coat to rest after lunch, with the sun shining brightly on her fair face. Ernest went off to get a tip on a horse and found a tout who gave him two horses to bet on. He put down half the money they brought with them on the first horse who won by four lengths. He tucked his winnings away for safe keeping and bet the second half of their gambling stake on horse number two, who managed to hold off the favorite and win by a whisker at the finish line. The first horse paid twelve to one and the second eight and a half to one. Ernest and Hadley celebrated with a glass of champagne at the bar under the stands.

"My, but racing is very hard on people," said Hadley. "Did you see that horse come up on him?"

"I can still feel it inside me," he said.

Now they had enough of a stake to live on for a while so Ernest could devote most of his energy and time to a novel he had started.

Ernest and Hadley bet on the horses a few more times after that with part of their winnings, celebrating their successes with champagne or a bottle of Sancerre, oysters on the half shell, or *crabe Mexicaine*. Ernest felt they were on a roll, luck was on his side, and soon he would be able to finish his novel and have a great success.

But despite feeling good about their winnings at the track, the Restaurant Michaud was still beyond their reach. As Ernest and Hadley passed Michaud's one evening, they peered in through the window and saw James Joyce dining inside with his wife Nora, their son Giorgio, and daughter Lucia. Joyce squinted at the menu through his small, thick eyeglasses, his lank hair combed straight back from his forehead. He held the menu close to his nose so he could read the print more clearly.

Ernest had told Sylvia Beach that it was impolite to stare at people when they were eating, but he thought it was fine to stare at Joyce through the window unobserved from the sidewalk outside. Joyce was the true gen, the true true gen, who wrote true sentences, some of the truest Ernest had ever read. But he always remembered not to mention his name in front of Gertrude, because she resented Joyce for writing some sentences that were even more incomprehensible than her own.

Chapter Four

"Did you see me cut him?" Ford Madox Ford asked Ernest. Ford was positively bubbling over with exhilaration.

"No. Who did you cut?"

"Belloc," said Ford. "*Did* I cut him!"

"I didn't see it. Why did you cut him?"

"For every good reason in the world. *Did* I cut him though!"

The writer Hilaire Belloc had just strutted past their table on the sidewalk outside the café. He was gaunt, wearing a cape, accompanied by a tall woman. He appeared to take no notice of them as he strolled down the boulevard.

Ernest had been sitting at a table in the Closerie des Lilas by himself when Ford entered and asked if he could sit with him. Ernest had resented Ford ever since the older man started to publish his stories at a time when Ernest desperately needed his patronage. Ford would forever be a reminder that Ernest *owed* him, that Ernest was not always the heavyweight champion of American writers and depended on support from others in his youth. There was nothing to be done about it now. Ford had already sat down before Ernest said it was OK.

Ford was a big shambling man with a stained bushy mustache. He had the eyes of a rummy, pale blue, washed out and bleary from years of imbibing too much. He ordered a brandy and soda from the waiter—a *fine a l'eau*. He gave off a musty smell of unwashed clothes, bad breath, and stale body odor. When the waiter brought his drink, Ford scowled at it and said, "I ordered a Chambery vermouth and cassis."

"I'll take the *fine*," said Ernest, taking pity on the waiter. "Bring Monsieur what he orders now."

"What I *did* order," Ford corrected him.

Ernest felt bad that Ford had been rude to Belloc, since Ernest had a high regard for Belloc as someone who had never crossed him in any way or tried to do him a favor. In fact, Ernest wouldn't have minded meeting Belloc if Ford had been civil to him and invited him and his companion in for a drink.

"What are you drinking brandy for?" Ford asked Ernest. "Don't you know it has led to the downfall of many young writers?"

"I don't drink it very often," said Ernest. At one time Ernest looked up to Ford, but he only felt sorry for him now. The man was a wreck, a caricature of his former self. He asked Ford again why he had cut Belloc.

"A gentleman will always cut a cad," said Ford.

"Would he cut a bounder?"

"It would be impossible for a gentleman to know a bounder."

Ernest shrugged. He was getting tired of playing with Ford's mind, tired of his silly banter. Ford ordered another brandy and soda from the waiter and drank it this time when the waiter brought it. After Ford left, a friend of Ernest from the races came over and took Ford's place at the table. Ernest saw Belloc walking back again in the other direction with the tall woman.

"That's Hilaire Belloc," Ernest said to his racetrack friend.

"Don't be a silly ass," the other man said. "That's Alestair Crowley, the diabolist. He's supposed to be the wickedest man in the world."

* * *

Ernest went back to the races at Auteuil and Enghien several times by himself after he finished writing in the mornings. Hadley didn't complain about his gambling or about being left alone with Bumby, since she knew he needed to complement their income until he finished his big novel and made a name for himself. Most days he did all right, winning enough to put a little extra money aside, but then one day it got to be too much. The gambling was getting in the way of his true calling, writing a great novel. Mostly it was the *thinking* about the horses, worrying about whether the horse that was *supposed* to win would actually come in first that crowded out the ideas he wanted to write about. He had reached a point where he was trying to earn his living as a gambler but calling it by another name. Either he was going to be a real writer, one who made his living at it, or else he was a phony. He decided he was not going to bet any longer. It had been a new and fine thing for quite some time, but now it was over.

It was not the true gen.

His luck with the writing suddenly took an unexpected turn. While visiting Sylvia Beach at Shakespeare and Company one afternoon, she handed him an envelope that felt as though it contained some money. "Wedderkop left it," she said.

"It must be from *Der Querschnitt*," said Ernest, referring to a German magazine that had apparently accepted some of his stories. "Did you see Wedderkop?"

"No."

Ernest opened the envelope. "It's six hundred francs. He says there will be more. It's damned funny that Germany is the only place I can sell anything. To him and the *Frankfurter Zeitung*."

"Don't you worry. You can sell stories to Ford," she said mischievously, knowing his sore spot.

"Thirty francs a page." Already he was pissed at writing for chump change, now that the Germans were more generous.

"But, Hemingway, don't worry about what they bring now. The point is that you can write them."

"I know I can write them, but nobody will buy them. There is no money coming in since I quit journalism." He failed to mention Hadley's trust fund income, which paid most of the bills.

He felt like a phony, complaining about his financial circumstances after quitting journalism of his own accord. There was only one remedy for that. He had to go out and have a drink. He left Sylvia and went over to Lipp's where he ordered a *distingue*—a liter of beer—and a bowl of potato salad. The beer was cold and wonderful and fine. And the potato salad was firm and marinated with olive oil. Ernest ground black pepper over the potato salad and mopped up the olive oil with bread. Then he ordered a *cervelas*—a thick sausage like a frankfurter split in half and smothered in a special mustard sauce. He ordered another *distingue* and drank it slowly.

Suddenly life was fine and true. To hell with Ford and to hell with the Germans. Soon he wouldn't need any of them. Soon he would be better than all of them and he would be able to cut them down to size when he thought they deserved it.

* * *

Ezra Pound wanted Ernest to teach him how to box. Ernest had great respect for Ezra at the time, before Ezra became crazy and anti-Semitic and started broadcasting propaganda for Mussolini. He lived in a ramshackle studio on the rue Notre-Dame-des-Champs with his wife Dorothy, who was pleasant and talented. Ernest liked Dorothy's looks as well and thought she had a beautiful body, but he never admitted that he wanted to fuck her.

Dorothy had short hair.

Ezra could be crotchety and irascible at times, but Ernest thought his poetry was pitch perfect when he hit it just right. Ernest had no need to cut Ezra down to size since Ezra was a poet and Ernest was primarily a prose writer, so he therefore didn't regard the older writer as a competitor. Ernest took pity on Ezra in the ring, teaching him moves and trying to make him look good instead of sucker-punching him in the face when his guard was down. While Ernest was sparring with Ezra, a nasty-looking man walked in wearing a wide-brimmed black hat that half-shielded his face, which looked like the face of a frog. The man had the eyes of an unsuccessful rapist. Ernest hated the man on sight and was even more appalled when Ezra introduced him to Ernest as Wyndham Lewis, the well-known British painter and novelist. Ernest wanted the man to go away, but he just hung around unpleasantly, egging Ernest on, hoping to see him thrash poor Ezra into a pulp. Ernest resisted the temptation and danced around the ring with Ezra, making him look good in front of Wyndham Lewis who observed them with a malevolent look in his eyes.

"I met the nastiest man I've ever seen today," Ernest said to Hadley when he returned home later.

"Tatie, don't tell me about him. Please don't tell me about him. We're just going to have dinner."

Ernest needed to talk to someone about the nasty painter and novelist, so he brought him up when he visited Gertrude a few days later.

"I call him the measuring worm," said Gertrude. "He comes over from London and he sees a good picture and takes a pencil out of his pocket and you watch him measuring it on the pencil with this thumb. Sighting on it and measuring it and seeing exactly how it is done. Then he goes back to London and does it and it doesn't come out right. He's missed what it's all about."

Ernest thought about that for a while and liked what she said. Gertrude had a gift for sizing up other people and putting her finger on their weaknesses, even as she was oblivious to her own. He wondered what it was about the man that Ezra found so engaging. Ezra was such a good and decent person who wouldn't seem to have anything in common with a man who looked like a frog, a man with the eyes of an unsuccessful rapist. But then again, Ernest hadn't seen Ezra's dark side yet, the side that led him to make radio broadcasts in support of one of the vilest political regimes in modern history.

Chapter Five

Ezra invited Ernest and Hadley to a party at his flat on the rue-Notre-Dame-des-Champs. Hadley thought that Ezra's wife Dorothy was truly beautiful. Her maiden name was Shakespear—without an e on the end—and her father claimed to be a remote descendant of the bard. Dorothy's mother had been William Butler Yeats's mistress. Dorothy was an artist of some note, and she and Ezra made no secret of their bohemian, counterculture marriage.

"Ezra and I have a wonderful relationship," Dorothy told Hadly. "But you must understand, it's not the same kind of relationship you and Ernest have."

Hadley doubted that Dorothy and Ezra even slept together, although he kept a mistress and was known to proposition just about any woman who captured his fancy. "Ezra and I sort of liked each other," said Hadley. But despite his bohemianism, Ezra was a misogynist to the marrow. "Ezra had funny ideas about women's brains. He didn't think we had any. So, of course, none of mine came forth when we were together."

While their flat was a bit on the shabby side, the main room was huge and sunny, decorated with paintings by Japanese artists. Ezra held court seated in an easy chair drinking Chinese tea while his guests—his subjects so to speak—gathered on the floor around his feet. He was fifteen years older than Ernest and had already established a reputation as a major poet and an *enfant terrible*—along with Gertrude—of Paris's expatriate literary community. He took an early interest in Ernest's work and offered to show it around to friends at *The Dial*, an American magazine specializing in modern literature. Ernest was flattered by the attention, and he maintained cordial relations with the older man for years, notwithstanding Ezra's attempts to help him advance his writing career.

"Ernest was always sweet to Ezra, who was more irascible than Ernest ever was," said Hadley.

Ezra, despite his generous and outgoing nature, took some getting used to. In the words of the writer Cynthia Ozick, Ezra was "idiosyncratic, noisy, cranky, aggressive, repetitively and tediously humorous, and perilously unpredictable." He seemed to have an inner need to "… shepherd movements, organize souls, administer lives."

No one was more surprised than Ernest and Hadley when Dorothy—whom Hadley regarded as essentially asexual—conceived on a trip to Egypt without Ezra. Ezra's mistress, Olga Rudge, had given birth to their son five months earlier, and now Dorothy would soon deliver a son of her own. Neither Ezra nor Dorothy thought there was anything odd about the situation, although Ernest was more than a bit jealous of Dorothy's fling in Egypt.

"He thought she was wonderful and beautiful and was half in love with her," Hadley admitted.

* * *

It was all but inevitable that Ernest's relationship with Gertrude would finally come to an end—although there is a question about exactly when and why the split took place. According to Ernest, the breakup centered on a quarrel he overheard between Gertrude and Alice. Ernest and Gertrude had become great friends and confidantes even though Ernest believed that it was virtually impossible to be friends with women writers who were just as ambitious as he was. Gertrude reciprocated Ernest's affection and gave him the run of her house.

"Hemingway," she said, "you have the run of the place. Don't you know that? I mean it truly. Come in any time and the maidservant will look after you and you must make yourself at home until I come."

So one bright, sunny afternoon, Ernest stopped by to visit after a walk along the Place de l'Observatoire past the little Luxembourg. The horse chestnut trees were in full bloom and children played on the gravel walks with their nurses sitting on the benches. Wood pigeons sung in the trees. It could not have been a more pleasant afternoon.

The maidservant opened the door for Ernest, made him a drink, and Ernest immediately heard the shouting emanating from upstairs. Alice was screaming at Gertrude in a ferocious manner, a manner in which Ernest had never heard one human being addressing another in his life. This was followed by Gertrude's plaintive voice, begging Alice in a demeaning tone that Ernest had never thought possible for the imperious writer.

"Don't, pussy. Don't. Don't, please don't. I'll do anything, pussy, but please don't do it. Please don't. Please don't, pussy."

Ernest turned to leave, but the maidservant tried to restrain him. "Don't go. She'll be right down."

But Ernest was truly shaken. The exchange between the two women had rattled him to the core. He uttered an excuse to the maid and left the apartment abruptly, knowing he would never come back.

Ernest returned to his apartment above the sawmill in a grim mood. When Hadley asked him what was wrong, he told her that he had inadvertently witnessed a shocking lovers' quarrel between Gertrude and Alice in their upstairs bedroom. "Ernest said he'd never heard such language," said Hadley.

"I'm just not going to have anything to do with them anymore," Ernest told her. He was too upset to even discuss the vivid details.

That was Ernest's version of what took place. Other accounts have it that Gertrude got upset with Ernest later, in the fall of 1926 when she heard he was leaving Hadley for another woman. Gertrude put the word out that Ernest was persona non grata at her flat. She would pretend she was not at home when he dropped by. It was at that point that Ernest decided her work was not all that good anymore and he parodied her in one of his sketches.

"And now it is all over about a very great writer who had stopped writing because she was too lazy to write for other people because writing for other people is very hard because other people know when things do not come out right and are failures…Gertrude Stein was never crazy. Gertrude Stein was very lazy."

Sweet, sweet revenge.

* * *

It was pleasant in the beginning after Ernest met F. Scott Fitzgerald for the first time at the Dingo bar on the rue Delambre. But it wasn't long before the relationship started to sour. Ernest considered Fitzgerald to be something of a threat, someone who might write a better novel than he ever would, and soon after he met Fitzgerald's wife Zelda, Ernest decided that he couldn't abide her.

"Don't tell Scott where I live," Ernest told Morley Callaghan, who arrived in Paris later.

"Why not? He worships you."

"Scott's just a rummy," said Ernest. "And Zelda is crazy."

"What do you mean?"

"She's just plain crazy. That's all there is to it."

Zelda, for her part, thought Ernest was a phony. And she resented Scott's infatuation with the short-story writer and budding novelist. "You're a fairy," she told her husband. "You'd rather go to bed with Ernest than sleep with me."

She must have been a delight to live with.

Ernest and Hadley had been dining at the Dingo with friends, some worthless characters really as Ernest described them, when Scott walked in and sat down at the polished mahogany bar. The bartender pointed out Ernest to him, and Scott sauntered over to his table and introduced himself. "There are only two people in Paris I want to meet," said Scott. "You and Jean Cocteau."

Ernest invited Scott to sit down with them. Scott's third novel, *The Great Gatsby*, had been published in April 1925 to generally good reviews but poor sales, which upset him terribly. Fortunately, the short stories he wrote for magazines brought in good money, but Scott and Zelda were spending it faster than it was coming in. Ernest, at that point, had published only a handful of short stories, and a full-length book of short stories, *In Our Time*, was scheduled for release by Boni and Liveright later that year. Yet, from the start, Scott was deferential to Ernest who was a few years younger and had yet to achieve Scott's renown with a novel of his own.

Ernest observed Scott carefully as the novelist sat down and launched into an embarrassing monologue about what a great writer Ernest was. He struck Ernest as somewhere between handsome and pretty. Scott was slightly built, so there was no need for Ernest to challenge him to a boxing match. He had wavy blond hair, light eyes, a thin straight nose, and a delicate rosebud of a mouth. He was a little drunk on champagne, tanned, ingenuous, somewhat out of place in his new surroundings. After a while, Hadley grew bored with Scott's monologue and embarrassed about his obsequious behavior toward Ernest even though Scott was the older and, so far, more accomplished writer. She told Ernest she was going home and left with the other dinner companions—her worthless friends.

Finally, after a sip of champagne that seemed to put Scott over the edge, his face turned a ghastly pallor as though he had been poisoned, and his manner became more aggressive. He began to interrogate Ernest with personal questions.

"Did you and your wife sleep together before you were married?" he demanded.

Ernest, who was no stranger to strong drink himself and recognized the various stages of inebriation as they evolved, grew wary and said simply, "I don't know."

"What do you mean you don't know?"

"I don't remember."

"But how can you not remember something of such importance?"

"I don't know. It is odd, isn't it?" said Ernest, playing with Scott's mind now.

"You could make an honest effort to remember," said Scott. Just then, Scott's face seemed to change into a death mask. His skin turned ghastly pale and shrank tautly over his cheekbones. His eyes grew flat and lifeless, becoming little more than dark holes in his face.

"Are you all right?" Ernest asked. Scott lowered his face onto the table like a small child and promptly passed out. Ernest was truly alarmed now. Here was a man who clearly should not drink at all, thought Ernest. The novelist's transformation had been virtually instantaneous, first nothing out of the ordinary, then total collapse a heartbeat later. Ernest lifted Scott out of his chair and trundled him out of the café onto the street. The taxis were lined up along the curb. Ernest lowered him into the back seat, where Scott fell over like a rag doll completely unconscious. Ernest had little choice but to take him home to Zelda.

Chapter Six

Hadley read *The Great Gatsby* before Ernest did and told him he should read it. "It's good," she said. "You read it and see."

Ernest, however, was thinking more about Zelda than about his new friend's novel. After seeing her for the first time, he admitted that he did not like her but he had an erotic dream about her. "The next time I saw her I told her that and she was pleased. That was the first and last time we ever had anything in common."

That was Ernest being a prick again; telling your friend's wife that you had an erotic dream about her was the same as telling her you wanted to fuck her. You didn't need to beat somebody up in the ring if you could cuckold him in his wife's mind.

Zelda was "a lovely and charming southern girl," said Hadley. "I enjoyed looking at her. But Ernest decided right away that first time he met her that she was crazy." Ernest wrote that he was struck by her "golden blowsiness." He liked the "tawny smoothness of her skin, the lovely color of her hair, and her shapely legs. But most of what she said did not make good sense to me. I did not like her."

Ernest *was* impressed by Scott's novel when he got around to reading it and respected the talent of the man who had written it. He decided that he wanted to see Scott again, even if it meant having to put up with Zelda and her distracting lunacy—a woman whom he did not like and thought was crazy but found erotic enough to dream about. But it wasn't too long before both Ernest and Hadley began to have second thoughts about this budding friendship. Ernest was a drinker who liked to boast about his ability to hold alcohol. But he was disciplined enough at the time to know when to turn the spigot off so that he had a clear head when he got up to write in the morning. Both Scott and Zelda, however, were out-of-control rummies—co-dependent enablers in the psychobabble of the late-twentieth and early twenty-first centuries—who fed each other's weakness for the western world's favorite mind-altering substance.

The Fitzgeralds started to show up at the Hemingways' apartment at the crack of dawn after a night of heavy drinking. "That used to happen a lot," said Hadley. "They would come at these outlandish hours after drinking, and they did foolish things like taking a roll of toilet paper and standing at the top of our stair landing and unraveling it all the way down." Ernest and Hadley detected immediately that Zelda was jealous of Scott's burgeoning celebrity and resented playing second fiddle to him. She regarded herself as an artist in her own right, and Ernest believed she deliberately wanted to keep Scott boozed up every night so that he couldn't get back to work on a new novel.

"She craved to show she had talent," said Hadley. "She needed to feel that she could do something as well as Scott." She tried to paint, studied ballet obsessively, and even tried her hand at writing. When Scott attempted to sober up and get back to work, Zelda called him a "killjoy" and "spoilsport." She flirted with other men and threatened to go out to parties on her own, so that Scott had to tag along against his better judgment to keep an eye on her.

Yes, she was an absolute delight to live with.

* * *

Ernest was trying to save enough money to go to Pamplona for the *feria* and watch the running of the bulls in July. Boni and Liveright had paid him a two-hundred-dollar advance for *In Our Time*, which was scheduled for release in the fall of 1925. Aside from the advance, Hadley's trust fund income, and the money he had saved from his racetrack winnings, there was not much left in reserve.

Ernest was also anxious to finish a longer work, a full-length novel, which would solidify his reputation as the premier American novelist of his generation. But Scott threw a new obstacle in his way when he asked Ernest to accompany him on a trip to the south of France to retrieve an errant automobile. Scott and Zelda had been forced to abandon their small Renault in Lyon on one of their trips, and he thought it would be fun for him and Ernest to take the train down and drive back to Paris together.

Ernest agreed to go, and Hadley thought it would be a fine thing for the two writers to get away for a couple of days and discuss writing and books without anyone else along. Ernest arrived at the Gare de Lyon at the appointed hour and waited for Scott, who had purchased their tickets and agreed to cover their expenses for the excursion.

Where was Scott?

Ernest waited and then waited some more, growing increasingly anxious that another all-night bender may have put Scott down for the count. This was *Scott's* outing after all, and he had only asked Ernest to come along for the ride and for the pleasure of Ernest's company. Without admitting it, Ernest had also thought that he might be able to glean something from the experience, perhaps learn something from an older, successful writer who already had three novels to his name. In his retelling later, though, Ernest talked about the journey as an act of charity he was conferring on a friend.

Still no Scott!

Now Ernest was really getting anxious. What to do, what to do if Scott didn't show?

Scott didn't show. Ernest had a decision to make: should he forget about the trip and go home, or should he buy a ticket for himself with money he couldn't afford to spend and head south without Scott? Ernest made up his mind. He got the name of a hotel in Lyon and wired Scott, telling him where to meet him when he finally arrived. Ernest had a short enough fuse as it was, and his temper was ready to explode by the time the train was heading south. "I had never heard, then, of a grown man missing a train," Ernest wrote. "But on this trip I was to learn many new things."

A bottle of wine goes a long way toward dispelling one's anger, so Ernest kicked back, observed the lovely French countryside whirring by, and enjoyed a fine bottle of St.-Emilion with his lunch. When he reached Lyon, he checked into the hotel and called Scott at his apartment in Paris. Zelda was indisposed, still sleeping off her hangover late in the afternoon after the excesses of the previous night, but the servant informed Ernest that Scott indeed had left Paris on a later train to Lyon. No, monsieur, he did not leave word where he would be staying. Now Ernest's anger started to boil again. How could a grown man not only miss his train but fail to leave some explanation of why he did, when he would be arriving, and where he would be staying? Was it possible that he didn't even *remember* that he had invited Ernest along in the first place?

Ernest had no choice but to go out for another drink, an *aperitif,* and vent his rage at the first stranger he ran into. If he stumbled across Scott by chance, he would have to restrain himself from wringing his neck like an androgynous chicken. The man was thoroughly self-centered and inconsiderate. And his wife was crazy, even if Ernest had dreamed about fucking her.

Ernest had a drink with a circus performer, a man who ate fire for a living, at a local café. He decided that the performer was amusing enough to spend some time with, so Ernest invited him to dinner at an Algerian restaurant, which served good food and drinkable Algerian wine. The man had no teeth and gummed his food with great efficiency. He was clearly someone who had learned to compensate for his failing. When Ernest told the toothless performer that he would soon have a book of short stories published, the man offered to tell him about some of his extraordinary adventures so Ernest could write them down in return for whatever amount of money Ernest could afford to pay him. The man evidently had many tales to tell about violence, debauchery, war, and various wicked customs that he had experienced first-hand during his global travels. Ernest paid the bill and told his dinner companion that they would meet again. He left him sitting there hunched over a drink, gumming his dessert, and went back upstairs to check on Scott again.

Still no word from the infuriating novelist. Ernest retired early, trying to keep his smoldering anger from erupting while reading a book by Turgenev, whom Gertrude did not think was *inaccrochable* even though he was a dead man like Aldous Huxley. Not that Ernest cared any longer what Gertrude thought about anything.

* * *

In the morning while Ernest was shaving, trying not to imagine Scott's face in the mirror for fear of drawing his razor too heavily across his own jugular vein, the desk clerk called to tell him that a gentleman was there to see him.

"Ask him to come up please," said Ernest.

When Scott failed to show up by the time Ernest had finished shaving, Ernest's mood grew darker yet. He debated with himself about whether he should challenge Scott to a boxing match despite the novelist's diminutive stature, but one look at Scott in the lobby moved Ernest to something approaching compassion. The smaller writer looked positively miserable. He had already consumed his first drink of the day, early as it was, and he stood there, hat literally in hand, trying to come up with a suitable apology.

"I'm terribly sorry there was this mix-up," said Scott. Then, incredibly, he shifted the blame for the entire fiasco from himself onto Ernest.

"If I had only known what hotel you were going to it would have been simple."

Ernest did not tell him that he had left word of where he was staying with Scott's maid, who said she would pass it along to Zelda when she woke up.

"I've been hunting all over the town for you," Scott added.

Ernest remained silent as long as he could, not sure what would come out of his mouth if he tried to respond. Finally he said, "Didn't they tell you at home that I was here?"

"No. Zelda wasn't feeling well and I probably shouldn't have come. This whole trip has been disastrous so far."

Ernest's fury began to dissipate. He realized he was in the company of a psychological invalid rather than a mature individual capable of making rational decisions.

"Let's get some breakfast and find the car and roll," said Ernest.

Scott insisted on eating at the hotel rather than at a café, where the food would have been better and cheaper. He then had the waiter make them a picnic basket for lunch on the road, even though Ernest suggested that they buy some local wine in Macon along with some bread, cheese, and chicken, instead of spending five times as much for the same items at the hotel. Scott had offered to cover their expenses, but Ernest had second thoughts about that arrangement and decided to pay his own way to put them on equal footing. Scott's extravagance was doubly annoying since he knew Ernest was hard up for money. After breakfast, they both had a whiskey and Perrier at the bar before setting out to retrieve Scott's Renault.

It was at the garage, after seeing the condition of the Renault that would convey them back to Paris, that Ernest suffered the biggest shock of the excursion so far.

"The car has no top," Ernest said, horrified.

"No. Zelda had it cut off," Scott said sadly.

"Why?"

"She hates tops," said Scott. "She can't stand tops on automobiles."

Chapter Seven

"You gentlemen have no waterproofs?" the mechanic asked
Ernest.

"No. I did not know about the top."

"Monsieur would not let me replace the top," said the mechanic,
gesturing toward Scott.

Scott was adamant about not letting the mechanic put a new top
on the car.

"Try and make the monsieur be serious," pleaded the mechanic.
"At least about the vehicle. One has an obligation to a vehicle."

He might as well have insisted that the monsieur give up drinking.
In addition, notwithstanding all the work the mechanic had done on the
car, Scott for some reason refused to let him change the piston rings. He
also couldn't guarantee the mechanic that he would make sure the
Renault had enough oil and water in the engine the next time he drove it.
His failure to keep the car properly lubricated had overheated it and
burnt the paint off the motor.

And so they set off on their motor trip back to Paris, stopping
every ten miles or so to escape the spring rains. They uncorked bottle
after bottle of the crisp, delicious wine of Macon, which they imbibed
virtually nonstop out of the bottles as they chugged their way north. Six,
seven, eight bottles of wine went down before and after lunch and during
their many rain stops. It was a merry adventure home, and after the
second or third bottle of wine, Ernest paid no heed to Scott's more
flagrant eccentricities, including his mounting hypochondria. The more
Scott drank, the more concerned he became about coming down with a
life-threatening illness such as congestion of the lungs. Ernest assured
Scott that the full-bodied white wine of Macon was the best medicine

known to mankind against the onset of pneumonia, but his prescription for good health failed to mollify the novelist. By late-afternoon, Scott declared that he was too sick to continue. He wanted to check into a hotel in the next town before fever and delirium totally overwhelmed him.

By the time they arrived at Chalon-sur-Saone, it was so late that all the pharmacies in town had shuttered their windows for the night. The two writers checked into a hotel. When they were ensconced in their room, they changed into their pajamas and sent their clothes down to be dried out. Scott was convinced that his death was imminent, and he could not rest until Ernest promised to look after Zelda and their daughter Scotty after he passed. It was important that he keep Zelda off the booze and make sure Scotty had an English governess.

"Look, Scott," Ernest said, "You're perfectly OK. If you want to do the best thing to keep from catching cold, just stay in bed and I'll order us each a lemonade and a whiskey. You can take an aspirin with yours."

Scott agreed that *citron presses* with two double whiskies would be good medicine. But he also insisted that Ernest order a thermometer from room service so that he could take his temperature to make sure he was not suffering from a congestion of the lungs. Ernest decided that Scott was not an alcoholic in the truest sense of the word since, notwithstanding their prodigious consumption of alcohol throughout the course of the day, a relatively small amount was all it took to either put Scott in a comatose state or else turn him into a raving madman. More likely, Scott was allergic to alcohol, which worked like a poison on his system.

Then again, Ernest may have been reinventing the definition of alcoholic to distance himself from its embrace.

Ernest finished the rest of a bottle of wine that he had uncorked in the car. The waiter finally arrived with their *citron presses* and whiskey, but he informed them that he had been unable to locate a thermometer at this hour of the evening. When he left, Scott glanced evilly toward the door and said, "They will only do something for you for a substantial tip. Most of them are rotten clean through."

By "them" he meant the French, and he elaborated on his theory that the Italians and the French were the lowest life forms on earth. He disliked the English as well, although he could tolerate them and sometimes looked up to them. After he had taken a few pulls from his double whiskey, he looked at Ernest and said, "You're a cold one, aren't you?"

"How do you mean, Scott?"

"You can sit there reading that dirty French rag of a paper and it doesn't mean a thing to you that I am dying."

"Do you want me to call a doctor?"

"No. I don't want a dirty French provincial doctor."

"What do you want?"

"I want my temperature taken."

With some difficulty, the waiter finally located a bath thermometer encased in a heavy block of wood overlaid with metal. "It is the only one in the hotel," said the waiter before beating a hasty retreat.

"You're lucky it's not a rectal thermometer," Ernest said to Scott with a hint of sadistic malice.

"Where does this kind go?"

"Under the arm."

Ernest demonstrated by sticking the bulky monstrosity in his own armpit first to get a reading. Then he did the same for Scott and left it there for a few minutes before making a great show of extracting it and studying the mercury level carefully.

"What is it?" asked Scott.

"The same as mine. Thirty-seven and six-tenths. It's a centigrade thermometer."

"That's normal?"

"Absolutely."

"Are you sure?"

"Absolutely sure."

Ernest couldn't remember if that was normal for centigrade, but it didn't matter because the thermometer was broken; the mercury level wouldn't budge off thirty no matter what Ernest did to it. The ruse worked like magic on Scott. He cheered up instantly and sat up in bed.

"We can be happy it cleared up so quickly," he said. "I've always had great recuperative power."

Scott wanted to celebrate his miraculous recovery by ordering more double whiskeys and *citron presses*. The waiter brought the drinks while they waited for their clothes to dry so they could go downstairs for dinner. Scott took the opportunity to unburden himself of some embarrassing details about Zelda's fling with a French aviator while they were on vacation in St.-Raphael a year earlier. Ernest listened intently as Scott told the story. His marriage to Zelda had been troubled from the beginning. She resented his talent and celebrity; she emasculated him sexually, even going so far as to have openly cheated on him; and she encouraging his drinking, knowing all the while that it got in the way of his writing. And yet he seemed to be addicted to her, and she to him. She was the most beautiful woman who had ever shared his bed—indeed, the only woman as he would confide to Ernest later—and he was her link to the glamorous world of literary fame.

*   *   *

The waiter brought two more double whiskeys and *citron presses* with their bundle of dry clothes. Ernest and Scott sipped them slowly while they dressed and then went downstairs to see what was on the menu. But first they needed a drink while they decided what to eat. Ernest ordered a carafe of Fleurie and an order of snails to start with. He assured Scott that the Fleurie was just as good a preventive against congestion of the lungs as the wine they had enjoyed earlier in the day. And the snails, of course, with lots of butter, garlic, and parsley, were just what the doctor ordered to go with the Fleurie—Doctor Hemingstein that is, as Ernest would jokingly refer to himself many years later after he became famous.

Scott was visibly woozy at this stage of the day, staring belligerently at the dirty, rotten French bastards who were scattered throughout the restaurant speaking their filthy provincial language. What were so many of them doing in here anyway? Then again, they *were* in France, so why would anyone logically expect to see a preponderance of some other ethnic type? Ernest told Scott that since they were still in a famous chicken region, they would most likely do well with the *poularde de Bresse*, washed down naturally with a bottle of Montagny, a delightful local white wine. Alas, before the chicken arrived, Scott lost consciousness and fell forward onto the table, doing a perfect face plant onto his napkin.

Ernest and the waiter carried the comatose novelist upstairs and stretched him out on his bed. Then Ernest returned to the dining room and finished his meal and the bottle of Montagny. Since Ernest was in training to become the heavyweight champion of American writers, he made it a practice not to drink any alcohol after dinner. So, the best way to deal with that brutal regimen was to stretch out the dinner hour well into the evening.

The next morning Ernest and Scott rose early and prepared to finish the final leg of their drive back to Paris. Scott was fully recovered and made no mention of the events of the previous day and night. Mercifully, the sun was bright and the air smelled fresh and clean as they headed north, so they did not have to worry about ducking out of the rain because Zelda did not like tops and had the roof cut off the car.

When Ernest arrived at his flat above the sawmill, Hadley greeted him effusively, happy to see him after his absence. "Did you have any fun or learn anything, Tatie?" she asked.

"I learned things I haven't sorted out," he said.

"Isn't Scott happy at all?"

"Maybe."

"Poor man."

"I learned one thing."

"What?"

"Never to go on trips with anyone you do not love. And we're going to Spain."

Hadley had also been anxious to see the running of the bulls again in Pamplona, which was less than six weeks away. She had enjoyed their earlier visits to the fiesta, even though Ernest had comported himself as though he were off on an adventure for guys only. But Hadley was beginning to have second thoughts about the trip this year. Ernest had been flirting more and more with attractive young women, and Hadley would have been content to skip what promised to be an unrestrained bacchanalia in Spain. Tatie, however, was determined to go.

Ernest thought hard about his misadventure with Scott and was willing to forgive him, realizing that anyone who could write a book as good as *The Great Gatsby* was exceptionally talented. Surely he would write an even better one someday.

Assuming that Zelda didn't destroy him first, that is.

Chapter Eight

And finally they were set to go to Pamplona. Hadley made arrangements for Bumby to spend a month with friends at their cottage in Brittany. They left Paris by train early in the morning and stopped first at Burguete on the Irati River, where they fished for trout—unsuccessfully this year, since the river had recently been polluted by lumbermen. On July 2, the first premonition of trouble in their marriage presented itself in the person of Lady Duff Twysden, whom Ernest had met—and possibly had an affair with. If he didn't, it wasn't for lack of desire.

"She had a certain grand vitality," Ernest described the fictional character based on her in his forthcoming book. "She was not supposed to be beautiful, but in a room with women who were supposed to be beautiful she killed their looks entirely."

Lady Duff exuded sexuality despite what some people described as her deliberately androgynous appearance. She sometimes wore a man's hat atop her cropped brown hair, bulky tweed skirts, and loose sweaters, but she was notorious for attracting any number of male admirers. She was clearly an alcoholic and lived with a man, a distant cousin, but cheated on him openly. Hadley had become increasingly concerned about Ernest's propensity for flirting with flamboyant, attractive women, especially when he was drinking, but had never suspected him of infidelity. She did, however, believe that he wanted to sleep with Duff.

Tall, slender, and witty, Duff had a bawdy sense of humor and a great capacity for drink. Lady Duff was notorious for treating men like library books, browsing through them before returning them late without paying a fine. Her eyes were a hypnotic gray, and several of her lovers described her as a blonde although one prominent suitor, the writer

Harold Loeb who spent a week in bed with her before Pamplona, said she was definitely a brunette. Ernest never forgave Loeb for sharing Lady Duff's bed and took his revenge shortly afterward in his novel.

"I was fond of Ernest before Pamplona," Loeb said. "Something happened then. I don't know whether it was because he liked Duff, or what. He took people that went on the fiesta to Pamplona and made a novel about them. I'm Jewish and I played tennis every day with him, so naturally readers connected me with the character Robert Cohn."

Both Harold and Ernest mooned over the infuriating Duff like schoolboys in heat throughout the fiesta.

"Harold Loeb will *never* get over the heartache that book caused him," said Hadley. "I've talked to him by the hour about Ernest and his ability to create composite characters. Almost none of his characters are pure Loeb or pure you or pure me. He makes a composite that fits his story. But I've never convinced Harold of that."

Ernest was ready for anything and everything when they arrived in Pamplona, high up in the hills of the northern province of Navarre. They checked into their room at the Hotel Quintana on the square in the center of the town. But Hadley's trepidations about the adventure only grew worse.

"It was a very upset summer for me," she said. "Ernest and I had not started to fall apart at that time. But everybody was drinking all the time, and everybody was having affairs all the time. I found it sort of upsetting. A lot of people thought Ernest had an affair with Duff. He just adored her."

Even before they left Paris, Ernest was at that point in a writer's life where the book he was meant to write, the great work he was *destined* to write, was boiling away inside ready to explode out of him and almost write itself. The urge and energy and basic framework were there; all he needed to do was immerse himself in his subject matter once again and then get it all down on paper in a white heat of literary fervor.

Channel it, so to speak.

But before the work begins, a writer has to give himself up to the madness of the moment and take possession of it, or let it take possession of him. And no one loved to party more than Ernest did. He was as caught up in the moment as anyone could possibly be. His description of the atmosphere in town was nothing short of euphoric.

"The godamnest wild time and fun you ever saw," he wrote to a friend. "Everybody in the town lit for a week, bulls racing loose through the streets every morning, dancing and fireworks all night…"

Afterword, Ernest wrote an article about the fiesta for the Toronto *Daily Star*: "The streets were solid with people dancing. Music was pounding and throbbing. Fireworks were being set off from the big public square…A rocket exploded over our heads with a blinding burst and the stick came swirling and whisking down. Dancers, snapping their fingers and whirling in perfect time through the crowd…"

Once the festivities got under way, Ernest and Hadley met up with the large cast of expats who served as the prototypes for the colorful characters in the novel he would soon write. Ernest's image as a man of action—war veteran, hunter, fisherman, outdoorsman—got a boost when a fellow writer and sometime bullfighter, Donald Ogden Stewart, cast Ernest in the role of a compassionate friend who came to his rescue after Stewart had been gored by a bull.

"My glasses flew in one direction, the cape in another, and I was tossed in the air amid a great gleeful shout from the spectators," he wrote in his autobiography. "When I hit the ground, however, an amazing thing happened. I lost my fear completely. And not only that—I got mad. I grabbed the cape and started to chase my enemy…Ernest clapped me on the back and I felt as though I had scored a winning touchdown. After we left the arena I discovered that a couple of ribs had been fractured, but that couldn't spoil the last frenzied night of drinking and dancing."

But when the story was reported in the *Chicago Tribune*, it was Ernest who had survived a near brush with death when the bull gored him while he was saving his friend Don Stewart from a mauling. As Canadian writer Morley Callaghan had said, Ernest had a gift for making people tell heroic stories about him, which only improved with each new embellishment.

* * *

Ernest and Hadley, who felt like an appendage during the fiesta while Ernest cavorted with their friends and flirted with Lady Duff, left Pamplona on July 13, 1925. They traveled around Spain and the Mediterranean coast for the next month or so while Ernest began work on *The Sun Also Rises*.

In a torrent of creative frenzy, Ernest pushed ahead with the first draft of his book. Hadley put on her game face and did her best to accommodate herself to Ernest's schedule, but it was a tense, and intense, stretch of weeks as Ernest lived his writing, and nothing but his writing, from day to day. He took only occasional breaks to look at paintings with Hadley at the Prado in Madrid, where they holed up for a time, but his heart wasn't in it. All he wanted to do was get back to his writing desk, to his work in progress that was now the sole purpose of his existence, his *raison d'etre*. For Hadley, the weeks dragged by sadly, with Ernest thoroughly consumed by the main passion of his life. He worked all day and sometimes at night until three or four in the morning.

"Then he would fall asleep, his head feeling like a frozen cabbage," Carlos Baker wrote in his biography of Ernest, "only to jump awake again a few hours later, with the words already stringing themselves into sentences, clamoring to be set down."

Hadley returned by herself to Paris on August 11, picked up Bumby, and waited for Ernest to come back a week later. Ernest continued his routine relentlessly, ruthlessly as it were, "working very hard," according to Hadley, disappearing every morning and night into his little room. When he finished the first draft on September 15, he was mentally exhausted but eerily elated, knowing he had done his finest work to date.

Lady Duff was featured prominently in the novel as Lady Brett Ashley; Ernest himself as reporter Jake Barnes; others whose names were not even disguised in the early draft—the only one missing from the story was Hadley. Hadley admitted to a friend that she was distressed "that I didn't see anything of myself in it." It was as though her husband had completely written her out of his life even as he included everyone else from their group in Pamplona. Partly to assuage his guilt for his weeks and months of neglect, Ernest presented Hadley with a painting by

Catalan artist Joan Miro for her thirty-fourth birthday and hung it over their bed at the sawmill as a surprise.

How did he afford it?

He borrowed heavily from friends that year, and even from Hadley, so that he could work nonstop on his book, convinced that it was destined to convey wealth and fame on him as soon as it saw the light of day. The Miro painting was more for himself than for Hadley, who was shocked by his extravagance. The price of the painting amounted to a month's living expenses for them.

"Have an idea we'll be making quite a little dough soon," he wrote a friend in one of his manic states. "Can feel it in the bones."

While he stopped for breath from his labor, he looked forward to the publication of his book of short stories, *In Our Time*, due out in October 1925. The reviews were mostly favorable but sales were puny. Ernest was upset when some critics compared his work to that of Sherwood Anderson who had just come out with a novel called *Dark Laughter*, a book Ernest considered silly and sentimental.

"There is something of Sherwood Anderson, of his fine bare effects and values coined from simplest words, in Hemingway's clear medium," stated a reviewer in the *New Republic*.

"With Sherwood Anderson and Ring Lardner this author shares a secret," said the Kansas City *Star*.

"There are obvious traces of Sherwood Anderson in Mr. Hemingway and there are subtler traces of Gertrude Stein," intoned a reviewer in the *Saturday Review of Literature*.

Ernest was so upset about the comparison that he commenced immediately to write a vicious parody of Anderson's book the same day. Hadley urged him to abandon the project, viewing it as a "detestable" cathartic step toward artistic independence, a betrayal of a friend who had helped Ernest get started a few years earlier. But Ernest would not be deterred. He worked away on the novella in another mad fury through Thanksgiving and completed the short venomous satire in ten days. He called his literary Declaration of Independence *The Torrents of Spring* when he published it the following summer, before *The Sun Also Rises* exploded into print. Ernest borrowed the title from Turgenev whom

Ernest discovered through Anderson, adding another twist to the horn Ernest gored into Anderson's hide.

Like Ford Madox Ford, Anderson had managed to get on Ernest's ugly side by doing him a favor. But there was method in Ernest's mad desire for revenge. Unhappy with the way Boni and Liveright had launched his book of stories, Ernest was determined to break his contract by presenting them with an unpublishable manuscript as his next book. He knew there was no way the publisher could bring out such a premeditated attack on one of their best-selling authors. His good buddy Scott had done Ernest the favor of talking up his work to Max Perkins, his own editor at Scribner's, and Ernest was anxious to make the switch to the better-known publishing house. For his part, Scott had encouraged Ernest to take a literary swing at Sherwood, telling him that the book was wonderfully funny and satire hurt no one. Little did Scott understand at the time how risky it was to help Ernest up the literary ladder of success.

* * *

On December 11, at the first sign of snowfall at Schruns in Austria, Ernest turned his attention back to *The Sun Also Rises.* Determined to polish the early chapters of the book before the year was over, he packed Hadley and Bumby up to the Vorarlberg near the Swiss and Italian borders for another stretch of concentrated labor, punctuated with afternoon runs down the slopes covered with two and a half feet of new snow.

A new "friend" entered their lives at that time—a young woman named Pauline Pfeiffer. Pauline spent her childhood in St. Louis where she attended Catholic schools and majored in journalism at the University of Missouri. Her family had money, quite a bit more than Hadley's family had. Pauline was small-boned and small-hipped, unlike the taller Hadley who looked as though she were born to rear children. She was attractive without being a classic beauty, and she had short hair and slim lines that made her look younger than the thirty she had turned on July 22, a day after Ernest's birthday. Here was another woman older than Ernest who caught his eye—this one by four years.

"We've been seeing a lot of Pauline Pfeiffer," Ernest wrote to a friend. Hadley remembered her as "…much more interested in the techniques of writing than I was." Ernest elaborated further in an experimental, unpublished fictional sketch he later wrote about her and himself:

"She was a nice girl and easy to talk to and said funny things and admired him…very much…and thought he was a fine writer and as his wife had bronchitis then and coughed a great deal and as [the girl] never coughed at all and seemed impervious to colds, even in Paris, and in a little while, without knowing it, through talk and having things in common and she being very attractive and admiring him to start with and he never having gone with any other woman before he was married and having been married now five years and she being such a nice girl at the corner he was in love with her."

Hadley was indeed sick much of the time during that early winter in Schruns, spending most of her time with Bumby while Ernest labored away on the second draft of *The Sun Also Rises*. Hadley's psyche was rapidly weakening. A more assertive woman would have sensed the stirrings in the air, and in her husband's loins, and sent the budding interloper packing. Pauline followed the couple and their child to Schruns, ostensibly to help Hadley shoulder the burden of de facto single parenthood while Ernest worked night and day with time out for little more than skiing. Pauline arrived on Christmas Day for a lengthy visit. Hadley had welcomed other women guests during the holidays before, but this Christmas season would be different.

She told a friend, "I *do* think I have a flaccid nature. I tend to give up before other people do."

Chapter Nine

Scott was upset about the size of his penis. Or rather, to put a finer point on it, he was upset that Zelda belittled him about the size of his penis. He needed a confidante, a buddy to run his problem past. So he picked Ernest—who would eventually tell the whole world about it in *A Moveable Feast*. God save me from my friends; my enemies I can deal with myself.

Shortly after Ernest returned from Pamplona, Scott invited him to lunch at Michaud's on the corner of the rue Jacob and the rue de Saints-Peres. He wanted to discuss something extremely important with Ernest and asked only that Ernest answered him as truly as he could. He wanted candor from Ernest, or so he said, even though when one answers a friend candidly it turns out that candor was not what the friend actually wanted and comes to resent such candor later on. Most often, people would rather hear exactly what they want to hear.

Ernest told him that he would do the best he could. He would give him the true gen, the true, true gen.

Scott drank wine at lunch, apparently his first drink of the day since he exhibited no signs of early morning imbibing. The wine appeared to have no effect on him. Scott was all business, discussing his latest book, the new novel he was working on despite Zelda's attempts to put him off his stride and off his writing game. Ernest listened and said little, wondering what this was all about, what was it that Scott wanted him to give the true gen about. For all outward appearances, they could have been two businessmen discussing tax and accounting issues over lunch. Finally, during dessert accompanied by a second carafe of wine, Scott broached the subject at hand.

"You know I never slept with anyone except Zelda," he said.

"No, I didn't"

"That is what I have to ask you about."

"Good. Go on."

"Zelda said that the way I was built I could never make any woman happy and that was what upset her originally. She said it was a matter of measurements. I have never felt the same since she said that and I have to know truly."

Not only was Zelda trying to put Scott off his stride, off his writing game; she was putting him off his stroke as well.

Ernest, glimmer in his eye, said there was only one way to know for sure. He told his buddy to follow him to *le toilet* where Ernest could get a close gander at Scott's pecker himself. Scott sheepishly followed his trusted buddy into the men's room where Ernest led him into *le cabinet* and scoped him out.

Back at their table, Ernest said, "You're perfectly fine. You are OK. There's nothing wrong with you. You look at yourself from above and you look foreshortened. Go over to the Louvre and look at the people in the statues and then go home and look at yourself in the mirror in profile."

"But why would she say it?"

"To put you out of business. That's the oldest way in the world of putting people out of business. This is the absolute truth and all you need. You could have gone to see a doctor."

"I didn't want to. I wanted you to tell me truly."

"Now do you believe me?"

"I don't know."

"It is not basically a question of the size in repose," said Ernest. "It is the size that it becomes. It is also a question of angle."

"But after what Zelda said…"

"Forget what Zelda said. Zelda is crazy. She just wants to destroy you."

That was too much candor. Scott wanted the true gen about his penis, but not about Zelda. Ernest had gone too far and now he had put Scott in a snit.

"You don't know anything about Zelda."

Ernest didn't mention it, but he did know that he once had an erotic dream about Zelda before he figured out how crazy she was. "Ernest, don't you think Al Jolson is greater than Jesus?" she had recently asked him apropos of nothing.

"All right," Ernest said. "Let it go at that. But you came to lunch to ask me a question and I've tried to give you an honest answer. Should we go and see some pictures."

"I'm not in the mood for looking at pictures," said Scott.

* * *

The *ménage a trois* continued through the holidays at Schruns into the early days of 1926. Pauline left Schruns on January 14 and returned to her writing job at *Vogue* in Paris. While Ernest was waiting for his ship to depart for New York to meet Perkins and sign a contract with Scribner's, and again on his return to Europe in March, he dallied in Paris with Pauline spending most of the time in bed with her in her fashionable Right Bank apartment. It was so much more elegant than the Left Bank dive he shared with Hadley and Bumby.

Hadley was there at the station to greet Ernest when he finally went back to the mountains. She had written to a friend telling her how much she missed her husband while he was away. Ernest was riddled with guilt.

"When I saw my wife again standing by the tracks as the train came in by the piled logs at the station," Ernest wrote, "I wished I had died before I ever loved anyone but her."

Well, maybe. But Ernest had been growing tired of Hadley for some time now, even before Pauline entered the picture. He had been flirting more and more openly with other women, not just Lady Duff, and was champing at the bit for a big change in his life to coincide with the publication of his first major novel.

Their rooms at the Hotel Taube were large and comfortable. The windows were wide and high, providing panoramic views of the broad valley and pristine snowfields, and the beds were piled with feather comforters. Down below was an inviting dining room and a warm wood-planked bar. These were the days before ski lifts were built in the area, so skiers trekked on seal skins strapped to the bottoms of their skis along logging trails that led up different valleys to the high mountain country. The seal skins were strapped on with the nap pointing downhill so that they gripped the snow when the skis slipped backwards. Up there at the ridge of the mountains the snow was untracked and virginal, blinding white under the Alpine sun. Skiers schussed over the high country above the trees, gliding over the passes and glaciers from one hut to another. Skiing was different back then than it is today; the spiral fracture was virtually unknown with basic bindings designed to snap off at the first sign of stress. Technology was supposed to be an improvement but has led to more serious long-lasting injuries today.

They ate and drank well at the hotel. The dollar was strong against most European currencies including the Austrian schilling at the time, and their rooms were cheap amounting to two dollars per day at the going exchange rate. They dined on jugged hare in a rich red wine sauce and venison in chestnut sauce and washed it down with light or dark beer and crisp white wine from the region. Ernest finished off his meal with a tart *kirsch* or *schnapps* made right there in the valley that burned like fire going down. Up in their rooms after dinner, they read books lent to them by Sylvia Beach.

Outwardly, then, all was tranquil as Ernest labored to complete his novel and deliver the final draft to Scribner's in New York. He was roiling away inside, however, a man in turmoil who was in love with two women at the same time—or rather, having an affair and falling in love with one woman while falling out of love with another.

"Schruns was a good place to work," Ernest wrote. "I know because I did the most difficult job of rewriting I have ever done there in the winter of 1925 and 1926, when I had to take the first draft of *The Sun Also Rises*, which I had written in one sprint of six weeks, and make it into a novel."

Then, in perhaps the most self-serving *apologia* for adultery ever penned by a major author, Ernest went on to blame his growing infatuation with Pauline on—well, on Pauline, the new woman who had entered their lives: "…an unmarried young woman becomes the temporary best friend of another young woman who is married, goes to live with the husband and wife and then unknowingly, innocently and unrelentingly sets out to marry the husband. When the husband is a writer and doing difficult work so that he is occupied much of the time and is not a good companion or partner to his wife for a big part of the day, the arrangement has advantages until you know how it works out. The husband has two attractive girls around when he has finished work. One is new and strange and if he has bad luck he gets to love them both."

Pauline's small breasts jiggled enticingly inside her blouse.

In the beginning, Hadley saw nothing of the handwriting on the wall. "Pauline was nice to me," she told a friend. "She wanted to be friends." But a bit later it was too late. "She didn't go straight for my husband," she said. "But once she made up her mind that he was what she wanted, she was very aggressive...She had the guts to spend a lot of violent energy on Ernest. He couldn't help himself."

With that remark Hadley established herself forevermore as the most understanding wife in history. Pauline's decision to go after Ernest was ironic in a way, since Pauline claimed to have been turned off at first by Ernest's bohemian dress style and the way he kept Hadley in borrowed clothes to skimp on money—her money. He cleaned up good though, and when he was clean-shaven and in trim fighting form, he was a magnet for various women.

"I liked Pauline," Hadley said. "I was a very poor young woman and Pauline was with the Paris office of *Vogue* and from the Hudnut family, which means money. Pauline's Uncle Gus owned Richard Hudnut Perfumes, Sloan's Liniment, and William Warner Pharmaceuticals. I didn't have any money because Ernest hadn't clicked yet."

Ernest finished the final draft of his novel in late April and mailed it to Max Perkins. Ernest's deception continued into the early summer. Finally, exasperated by her husband's foul moods and suspecting that Pauline was the cause of them, Hadley confronted Ernest directly. What was going on between him and Pauline, she demanded to know.

Ernest didn't exactly deny that something, indeed, was going on. But he also had a genius for transferring the blame to someone else—in this case Hadley. "I couldn't help it," he said. "It happened. It was happening, and there's nothing I can do about it. If you hadn't brought it out in the open, it would not have become a problem."

So Pauline had been responsible for Ernest's falling in love with her, and Hadley had created their marital problem by bringing up Ernest's infidelity

Soon he would be leaving her for Pauline. She had grown accustomed to his infatuations by now but never thought he would go this far. She never thought he would actually leave her. Hadley was crushed. Ernest was so despondent he thought of taking his own life, briefly. But there was the book, and the book was everything. There was the book, and now there was Pauline.

A new book, a new woman, a new direction in life.

Ernest was about to become a true literary star. It was time to leave the old life behind and embrace the new one. He could feel it in his bones. His time had come.

PART TWO

THE BELL ALSO TOLLS

Chapter Ten

Hadley wasn't going down without a fight. She had been married to Ernest too long to accept defeat so quickly. She and Ernest decided to separate while they sorted out their feelings. Ernest holed up in a flat lent to him by a wealthy friend, Gerald Murphy, and he hung Miro's painting on the wall in front of his writing desk to keep him company—the same painting he had bought Hadley for her birthday, with her own money. Hadley and Bumby moved to more spacious digs on the rue de Fleurus not too far from Gertrude and Alice.

Ernest was miserable living alone. He described his new surroundings in a sketch he wrote later as being "...at the end of a block of studios on a gravel courtyard. It was one big room with a cement floor and a skylight. There was a gas stove in one corner to cook on and in the other corner a stairway went up to a little platform built across one end of the studio where his bed and washstand were. There was a window and the washstand on the other side. A curtain separated the platform from the rest of the studio and made a room out of it. The walls were whitewashed."

It sounded Spartan except for the nights when Pauline was there to share his cramped new quarters. But she could not be there as often as she and Ernest would have wanted because Hadley threw a roadblock in the way of the lovers. Hadley would consent to give Ernest a divorce, she said, if he agreed not to see Pauline for one hundred days. If they still loved each other after one hundred days of separation, Hadley would not stand in their way. Hadley was convinced that Ernest would grow tired of his new paramour during that period and come running back to her and Bumby. It was another one of Ernest's infatuations, she told herself. He just *thought* he wanted to be free of her and Bumby. Hadley believed that a little more than three months without Pauline would cool his lust for her erstwhile friend.

Ernest and Pauline agreed to the terms—how could they not? But the only way they could stay away from each other for the hundred-day trial was for Pauline to physically remove herself from Ernest's proximity. She set sail for New York on September 24, 1926, and from there traveled to Piggott, Arkansas, where her parents had moved. Now Ernest was truly alone, separated from the woman he loved and, by choice, from the woman he used to love.

He looked forward to the publication of *The Torrents of Spring*, which Scribner's had reluctantly agreed to publish to acquire his first novel. And mostly he kept busy with the galleys of *The Sun Also Rises*, working diligently to strip out some of the profanities Max Perkins found offensive—the words *fuck*, *shit*, and *cocksucker* among others were targeted by the censors of the day. Ernest also eliminated the first fourteen pages of the original draft at the suggestion of Scott who thought the opening pages slowed down the story. Scott thought Ernest would fume at his suggestion, but Ernest took it well, trusting in his buddy's editorial judgment. When Ernest mailed the corrected galleys back to Max on August 27, his dedication page read:

"This book is for Hadley

And for John Hadley Nicanor"

Ernest directed that the royalties for the book go to Hadley and his son. His conscience was clear. He was paying for his infidelity with cold, hard cash. But his generosity left him broke. His fifteen-hundred-dollar advance from Scribner's was all but gone, and he depended on a loan of four hundred dollars from Gerald Murphy to pay his expenses. Ernest at the ripe old age of twenty-seven had already begun to call himself "Papa." Papa Hemingway. It was a way of showing that he was the top dog in command of his circumstances, even when it was obvious that he was not.

The Torrents of Spring sold poorly and was virtually forgotten as soon as it came out. Not so *The Sun Also Rises*, which was published in New York on October 22 to generally good reviews and slow sales at first, which picked up briskly during the next few months. The novel quickly developed a cult following, particularly among college kids who couldn't wait to visit Pamplona, get drunk, and run with the bulls or get trampled while doing it. Ernest's feeling in his bones that he was about to make some dough was right on the money. The book, at least, certainly made money for Hadley. The novel launched Ernest as the most talked-about young writer of his generation.

But not all the reviews were raves. One that irked him the most was written by his novelist friend John Dos Passos, who was more celebrated than Ernest at the time. Ernest's book was "extraordinarily well-written," Dos Passos wrote. But a novel needed more than style to carry it along. "Instead of being the epic of the sun also rising on a lost generation…this novel strikes you as a cock and bull story about a lot of summer tourists getting drunk and making fools of themselves in a picturesque Iberian folk-festival…It's heartbreaking. If the generation is going to lose itself, for God's sake let it show more fight…When a superbly written description of the fiesta of San Fermin in Pamplona…reminds you of a travel book…it's time to hold an inquest."

Ernest fumed at Dos's betrayal. The knowledge that he had done no less himself to his own friends, even going so far as to write a parody of one of their works, made no difference to him. But Ernest would have the last laugh. His novel caught on and his career eventually eclipsed and outlasted Dos's—Ernest's friend Dos, whose photo graced the cover of *Time* magazine when Ernest was still scrambling for recognition. The more some critics carped at Ernest's brutal portrayal of his friends, the more popular the book became.

"One of the protagonists (and what a savage portrait!) is easily recognized as one of Hemingway's literary pals," wrote a gossip columnist for the Paris *Herald*. "Several well-known habitués of the Carrefour Vavin are mercilessly dragged through the pages. Not very pretty reading, their recorded actions and reactions, but then Hemingway is noted for being an observant journalist and for not respecting the feelings of friends."

Everyone is turned on by gossip, particularly gossip about celebrities. The *Tribune* did its part to fan the flames of success with its own offering. "The person heard of as often as anyone is young Mr.

Hemingway, who apparently is arriving. It is now the right thing to mention his name casually, as if one had read his stories, and the cult is being founded. He is doing the really remarkable feat of making a reputation among his own countrymen out of his own country."

Ernest himself could not have said it better. Well, rather he could have expressed the thought more elegantly. But when it came to reviews, the substance not the style carries the day.

* * *

And then, unexpectedly, during the one-hundred-day separation she had imposed on her husband and Pauline, Hadley fell in love. In a delicious stroke of irony, Hadley not only fell in love, she fell in love with her best friend's husband. On the surface it appeared as though she were doing Ernest one better, pulling an "Ernest" as it were. But that was only on the surface. The reality of the situation was that Hadley's friend Winifred Mowrer had grown tired of her husband Paul and encouraged Hadley to take him up on his advances toward her if she were so inclined. As it turned out, Hadley was indeed inclined. She found Paul attentive, suave, and debonair. Within a trice Hadley found herself falling for him and was no longer interested in saving her marriage.

"The entire problem belongs to you two," she wrote to Ernest. "I am *not* responsible for your future welfare. It is in your hands and the hands of God…the three months separation is officially off."

Ernest and Pauline were free to do as they pleased, as Hadley was free to do as *she* pleased. Once she realized that her future and her happiness no longer depended on Ernest, Hadley felt as though a great weight had lifted from her shoulders. She became a different person overnight, laughing more, expressing her own thoughts more freely without wondering whether Ernest would agree with them or not, dressing better, growing more outgoing in social gatherings. Yes, she had set Ernest and Pauline free, and in doing so had unleashed her own individuality. Ernest lost no time in conveying the news to Pauline in a telegram:

THREE MONTHS TERMINATED AT HADLEY'S
REQUEST SHE STARTING IMMEDIATELY OWN REASONS
STOP COMMUNICATION RESUMED STOP SUGGEST YOU
SAIL AFTER CHRISTMAS WHAT ABOUT ME

To Hadley he wrote, "If you wish to divorce me, I will start at once finding out the details and about lawyers."

While Ernest waited patiently for Pauline to return to Paris, he spent most of his time writing new stories and reading reviews of his novel. Sales of the book mounted steadily, which would turn Hadley into a reasonably well-off woman. By the end of January 1927, it had gone into its fourth printing, with sales approaching eleven thousand copies. It was a Pyrrhic victory of sorts for Ernest because, while Hadley was counting the royalties that would soon start falling into her bank account, Ernest remained penurious and dependent on Pauline's money. In that regard his circumstances had not changed; he still depended on his women to pay his bills.

Chapter Eleven

On March 10 Ernest saw Hadley for the first time in months when they jointly signed their divorce documents, giving Hadley custody of Bumby and outlining their financial arrangements. The divorce would become official on April 14. Pauline and her sister Jinny accompanied Ernest to the lawyer's office. Ernest studied Hadley carefully, marveling at her chic new look, her fine new clothes, her changed demeanor and bubbly new personality as they signed the papers that would seal their fates. He felt a twinge of resentment at how liberated she looked.

Shouldn't she have been miserable now that their marriage was finally ending?

By this time Ernest had heard about Paul—Hadley's Paul. Ernest stood there simmering with his *Pauline* by his side, wishing that Hadley didn't look quite so effervescent on such a solemn occasion. To hell with it all, he thought to himself. He was getting what he wanted, but he didn't imagine that Hadley would get through this ordeal in such fine mettle, with another man in her life no less.

Ernest responded by leaving Pauline and Jinny in Paris to scout around for a larger apartment while he piled into a car with a friend, Guy Hickok, and took off on a motor trip through Italy. Guy pushed on at a feverish clip, squinting through his cracked windshield as he racked up more than two thousand miles in eleven days over muddy, unpaved, narrow roads. While he was gone, Pauline located a suitable flat for her and Ernest at 6 rue Ferou, a cobbled street filled with religious shops situated near the Church of St. Sulpice adjoining the Luxembourg Gardens. For the equivalent of thirty dollars a month, the flat came with a garden courtyard, a master bedroom and salon, dining room, kitchen, two small rooms, and two toilets. Ernest would be so pleased to see their new quarters when he returned. In a scene too reminiscent of Ernest's trip through southern France with Scott a while back, Guy's car broke down in Dijon. Disgusted with what had been for him a less than enjoyable vacation with Guy, Ernest left him there to deal with the problem and hopped a train back to Paris.

Ernest's financial problems did not last long. There was, of course, the not insubstantial income from Pauline's trust account to tide them over. Checks started arriving in short order from various members of Pauline's family amounting to a year's living expenses in Paris. On top of that, there was great demand from magazines for Ernest's short stories now that his novel had proven a success. *That* money, unlike royalties from the book, would be his and Pauline's to keep. Max Perkins was clamoring for a new novel from Ernest, but Ernest was putting together another book of short stories instead, which would be published with the title *Men Without Women*.

Ernest married Pauline twice on May 10—as was customary in France—first in a civil ceremony and a second time in a union sanctioned by the Catholic Church. Ernest became a Catholic, and his friends assumed that Ernest converted to please his new wife. But the truth was more complicated than that. In Italy during the First World War, Ernest had been spellbound by a nation in which religion was woven into every fiber of the culture. It was a country where men would make blasphemous jokes about the Church without actually leaving it. How different that was from his Midwestern Congregational upbringing saturated with hypocrisy, which fostered his father's unbearable piety and his mother's church politics about who ruled the choir loft. When Ernest was wounded by shrapnel, he received extreme unction from a priest who anointed his forehead with holy oil and mesmerized him with the mystery, ceremony, and ritual of the Catholic Church. He never forgot the medieval wonder of it all.

Before Ernest married Pauline, he had written to a friend declaring, "If I am anything I am a Catholic. Had extreme unction administered to me as such in July 1918 and recovered. So guess I am a super-Catholic...Am not what is called a "good" Catholic, but cannot imagine taking any other religion seriously."

* * *

Ernest finished correcting the galleys for *Men Without Women* on August 17, 1927, and mailed them to Max the same day. The book was published on October 14, the same month that Pauline discovered she was pregnant with their first child. When things are going well, it seems, they all go well together. Not that the book of stories met with universal approval from the literary mafia, who were waiting with daggers drawn to eviscerate Ernest's follow-up offering to his novel published a year earlier. Dorothy Parker and the reviewer for *Time* magazine loved the latest book, but others were less kind. Joseph Wood Krutch, an influential critic of the period, sniffed that Ernest wrote "sordid little catastrophes in the lives of very vulgar people."

Virginia Woolf wrote that Ernest was "self-consciously virile," and his stories were "a little dry and sterile." None of their barbs could stop the sales of the book, though, which caught on quickly with the same readers who gobbled up *The Sun Also Rises*. By early December, sales had already topped thirteen thousand copies. But Ernest was stung by the negative reviews nonetheless.

He wrote to Scott saying, "These goddamn reviews are sent to me by my 'friends,' any review saying the stuff is a pile of shit I get at least 2000 copies of."

Early the next year, Pauline started to pack up for a trip back to the states. Her baby was due in June and she wanted him or her to be born on American soil. Pauline's family had yet to meet Ernest, and now that his writing career had taken off she was anxious to trot him around back home. It was different than in the beginning when he was penniless, virtually unknown, about to leave his wife for another woman (her), and had little to show for his efforts except some short stories and a first novel in progress. Now she had a real story to tell and a rising literary star to put on exhibit.

Pauline thought that they could not get out of Paris fast enough. Not only had she inherited Hadley's husband when she married him, but Pauline inherited his social baggage as well. The list of the walking wounded whom Ernest left scattered over the literary battlefield as a result of his writing included just about everyone he knew. The list was long and impressive: Harold Loeb, Ford Madox Ford, Gertrude Stein, Robert McAlmon, Sherwood Anderson, Lewis Galantiere, Duff Twysden—the roster was endless. Pauline wanted to leave town before Ernest started in on *her* friends now that he had turned his own into road kill. But before she could get him out of Gay Paree, the roof quite literally fell in on him. The *Herald* reported the accident in March.

"Mr. Ernest Hemingway, author who was wounded about the head when a skylight crashed on him at his home Sunday morning, yesterday was recovering, according to officials at the American Hospital at Neuilly. Mr. Hemingway's wound, which required three stitches inside and six outside, is healing and he was able to pursue his usual life."

"I was there shortly after a skylight fell on his head," said writer Archibald MacLeish, another of Ernest's benefactors. "I think he'd probably had a good deal to drink and pulled the wrong rope in the can. I was the first one called. Someone dug up a tax at about half past two in the morning and I went around and picked him up and took him to the hospital. He'd lost a lot of blood by that time so that he babbled a good deal on the way to the hospital. He took a great many stitches with just a local anesthetic and he sat through the whole thing talking to the doctor, telling him the story of his life."

The look and smell of his own blood put Ernest back in World War I when a mortar blast turned his right knee into jelly. The war injury left Ernest with a slight limp, and the skylight accident would leave him scarred for many years afterward, but it turned out to be fortuitous in a significant way. For some time now he had been searching for a viable subject for his next novel, and now he had it. Not since he was a youth in the war had he seen so much of his own body flayed open like raw meat on a butcher's block. The war had been the most telling and traumatic experience of his life to date. Against Pauline's protests that he should heal first and then get ready for their trip, Ernest sat down and wrote the opening pages of a new novel. He didn't have his title yet, but it would come to him soon enough. It seemed almost inevitable that he would call it *A Farewell to Arms*.

And finally they left—but not immediately to Arkansas where Pauline's parents were anxiously waiting to greet their daughter and son-in-law. Ernest had always wondered if he could ever live back in the states again after immersing himself in the sights, smells, and wonders of Paris for several years. He had his answer as soon as he cast his eyes on Key West. Ernest and Pauline had gone there to pick up a new Ford given to them by Pauline's rich Uncle Gus, who managed her trust account.

Key West was the closest thing to a foreign country that Ernest had seen inside the country of his birth. On the surface the town was shabby and down on its heels at the time. But the flowering jacaranda trees, the explosion of scarlet bougainvillea, yellow cassia, and red-orange flame trees more than made up for the sun- and salt-blasted fishermen's shacks with weather-dulled paint peeling off like layers of old, parched skin. The local sponge beds were blighted, the cigar factories had been boarded up, and the naval base deactivated. But the local honky-tonk bars were lively and the air was filled with men who spoke everything from English to Caribbean Creole to Cuban Spanish and chose to ignore the infamous Prohibition laws. Key West was an outlaw town populated by rebels, and the Feds chose to ignore their open rebelliousness for fear of igniting an insurrection by men who would fight to the death to preserve their lifestyle.

Ernest fell in love with Key West at first sight. When the local inhabitants weren't drinking they were fishing, and when they weren't fishing they were drinking. Here was a place where he could write, fish, and drink and live life to the fullest if he ever chose to do so. Key West was made for him. The pregnant Pauline looked around her somewhat aghast at first. This was not exactly what she envisioned coming home to. But Ernest was in pig heaven.

Chapter Twelve

Ernest kept Pauline in Key West longer than she would have liked. He worked mornings on his new novel, fished in the afternoons with the locals, and drank with them in the evenings. The more she mentioned Piggott, Arkansas, to him, the more he dug in his heels. And the date of her expected delivery was drawing closer. Her family grew increasingly exasperated by their absence until Pauline's father Paul could stand it no longer. He was alarmed that his daughter, now in her eighth month of pregnancy, might have to give birth in such a hellhole as Key West. In mid-May he pounced on the errant couple without warning, put his daughter on a northbound train, and refused to leave until Ernest agreed to drive him back to Piggott in Uncle Gus's Ford.

Ernest had met his match in his father-in-law, a man as stubborn and willful as he was. Ernest was understandably reluctant to spend so much time cooped up in a car with the taciturn, disapproving Paul Pfeiffer. But he had little choice except to pack up the two hundred pages he had already completed on the novel, bid his fishing and drinking buddies farewell, and hit the road with Papa Pfeiffer. In Paris Ernest had been insulated from the demands of family, both his and Hadley's. Now that he was back on American soil he was about to learn that one doesn't marry just a person, one marries an entire family and all the obligations that go with it.

It took Ernest and Paul six excruciating days to cover the fourteen hundred miles from Key West to Piggott. Which of them had the more uncomfortable time during the journey is hard to say, for the two men clearly did not like each other. The drive was long, slow, and tedious along two-lane concrete highways that frequently gave way to packed gravel. It took them a full day just to drive out of the Keys since the road was broken at the time by a forty-one-mile ferry ride between No Name Key and Lower Matecumbe. At a time before ubiquitous motels were stretched across the length and breadth of the country, their nights were spent in hot, smelly tourist cabins in the woods along the roadside, many without electricity. When the odd twosome arrived in Piggott, the Pfeiffer's two-story home with its tree-shaded porches instantly reminded Ernest of Oak Park, Illinois, where Ernest had grown up and come to detest. The one saving grace for Ernest was Pauline's mother Mary, with whom Ernest bonded at once. He despised his own domineering, self-centered mother, whom he blamed for breaking the spirit of his docile father. Mary was quite the opposite: warm, loving, even a bit flirtatious with him in a maternal way. Mary was the mother he always wished he had.

For Ernest, the two weeks he spent in Piggott were stultifying. Paul Pfeiffer was less than impressed by Ernest's war stories and tales of life on the Left Bank of Paris, and he was not shy about showing it. The plan was for Pauline to deliver their baby in Kansas City, a two-day drive from Piggott, so as her due date drew closer Ernest couldn't wait to hit the road. And then Ernest became a father again when Pauline delivered his second son Patrick via caesarian section on June 28, 1928. Ernest immediately sent out a telegram to almost everyone he knew:

PATRICK NINE POUNDS ARRIVED RESEARCH HOSPITAL 7:30 TONIGHT STOP BOTH HE AND PAULINE BOTH WELL

Ernest's happiness over the event was soon dashed by his father, who mailed him a clipping from his hometown newspaper, *The Oak Parker*. The article read in part, "Ernest Hemingway, One of Ours, apparently doesn't have an ideal to his name and 'respectability' is not one of his literary traits. Still, Oak Park must accept him…because he is one of the acknowledged leaders in contemporary literature."

Thanks for sharing that, Dad.

Ernest was furious, but he knew that sooner or later he would have to make the obligatory trip home to visit his own parents, who were more than anxious to see their wandering son and meet his new wife and baby as soon as they were able to travel with him. But he wouldn't go there just yet. He drove Pauline and the baby from the hospital back to Piggott, arriving the day before Ernest's birthday on July 21 and two days before Pauline's. Then, while Pauline rested in the bosom of her family to recuperate from her caesarian delivery, Ernest took off with a buddy in the Ford for a hunting and fishing trip in Wyoming. The journey was grueling at the time, requiring a spare tire, a hand pump, and lots of inner tubes and patch kits to fix the frequent flat tires inflicted on cars by unpaved dirt and gravel roads. Their speed rarely exceeded thirty-five miles an hour.

The summer wore on slowly. Pauline pined for Ernest in Piggott while she regained her strength, and Ernest was enraptured by the wild western country where he could work on his novel, shoot wildlife, and pull fish out of the rivers to his heart's content. In mid-August Pauline wrote Ernest that her weight was back up to one hundred and eleven pounds and she was feeling fine. Ernest was feeling just fine too, thank you. Finally Pauline could take his absence no longer. If she wanted to see him soon, she would have to leave Patrick with her parents and go out where Ernest was. Only God knew when Ernest was planning to return since he was always vague about his itinerary, preferring to go here or there on the spur of the moment. Paul Pfeiffer put his daughter on the train, trying not to let his rage and disappointment show as he watched the metal monster carry Pauline away from him down the tracks. Already he was getting tired of seeing his daughter off on trains carrying her toward, or away from, her unpredictable husband.

* * *

They stayed out there for more than a month together, until Ernest finished the first draft of the novel. The horizon was way out there in the distance beyond the wide vistas of yellow grain, prairie grass, and herds of bison, cattle, elk, and sheep. They drove in their dust-layered Ford through the Big Horn Mountains over to Shell, farther west to Cody, over the Sylvan Pass into Yellowstone where the trees were already taking on their fall colors. And then…and then…they had to face the unavoidable. Ernest turned the Ford in an eastward direction and chugged slowly back to Piggott.

Pauline was not nearly as amused as Ernest was when Ezra Pound sent them a little throw-away ditty he wrote: "Wots the pig got? Wott got has the Pig got? Piggott mit uns!"

Ernest and Pauline arrived back in Piggott on September 25 in their beat-up, dirt-covered Ford, which looked as though Ernest had taken it on a combat mission. He stayed for a few days, making some revisions on the novel, and then deposited the six-hundred-and-fifty-two page manuscript in a safe deposit box in a local bank and made plans to head up north to Oak Park, Illinois, where his hometown audience believed that he had no ideals or respectability. He promised his folks that he would return with Pauline and Patrick as soon as they were able to travel.

Oak Park was different than he remembered it when he left nine years earlier. The vacant lots were gone, filled in with rows of flat-topped apartments. Late-model automobiles cluttered the streets. But the family homestead at 600 North Kenilworth had not changed a bit, and Ernest was overcome by a pall of despondency at the sight of it. He felt suffocated as though the confines of his childhood were closing in on him. The major difference he noticed inside the house was on the walls, covered now with his mother's oil paintings, which Ernest did not think exhibited much in the way of talent.

His mother Grace was as big as ever, bigger than life like her son, bubbly, overwhelming, full of herself and her imagined new career as an accomplished artist. His father Clarence was even more diminished than he had been a few years earlier. He was thin, gaunt, pale, and depressed by his disastrous retirement investments in Florida real estate, which had left the family in a precarious financial condition. On top of that, Clarence had recently been diagnosed with angina and diabetes. The family gathering included Ernest's younger sisters Ursula, Sunny, and Carol, and his fourteen year-old brother Leicester; Marcelline, the oldest sibling, could not make the trip from Detroit. Grace talked nonstop about herself and made Ernest promise to place her paintings with a salon or gallery when he returned to Paris.

Ernest endured the agony for five days. If he didn't break free of the ensnaring web immediately, he thought he might turn into a twelve-year-old child again occupying his old bedroom in his parents' house. He hit the road, leaving Oak Park behind for the next-to-last time as he drove to Chicago, planning to meet Pauline there. The Pfeiffers were getting to know their grandson well, caring for him for long stretches while their daughter raced off to different parts of the country to be with her husband. From Chicago Ernest and Pauline took the train to New York, where they hooked up briefly with Scott and Zelda and went to a football game in Princeton. Ernest had been on a whirlwind tour since their arrival in the states, maintaining a pace that could not continue indefinitely. Since leaving Paris, he had traveled to Key West to Piggott to Kansas City to Piggott to Wyoming to Piggott to Oak Park to Chicago to New York. It was almost as though he were running away from something rather than running toward a destination. And now he and Pauline were cementing further plans to travel back to Chicago to retrieve their Ford, from there to Piggott to Oak Park to Key West again before heading back to Paris.

* * *

But all was not to come off as planned. On December 6, 1928, Clarence rose early as usual in the bedroom of his Oak Park home. He went down to his basement where the furnace was roaring at full power. He pushed some personal papers into the inferno of the firebox, then went back upstairs to his bedroom. Clarence kept a loaded pistol there, an old .32 caliber Smith and Wesson revolver that his father had used as a union soldier during the Civil War.

The revolver still worked.

Clarence pressed the muzzle of the revolver behind his right ear. And then he pulled the trigger. The crack of gunfire resonated throughout the house. When Leicester found him sprawled on the bed, Clarence was still alive—but just barely. His head was all but unrecognizable in a spreading pool of blood. Leicester didn't know it at the time, but he was looking into his and Ernest's future. Ernest ended his life with a shotgun blast in 1961, and Leicester fired a bullet into his own brain in 1982 after his doctor told him he would have to have his legs amputated as a result of diabetes.

Ernest was on a train when he heard about his father's suicide in a telegram from his sister Carol.

FATHER DIED THIS MORNING ARRANGE TO STOP HERE IF POSSIBLE

When Ernest returned to Oak Park, Grace gave him the revolver that his father had used to take his life. Ernest later described it as Grace's sadistic gift to him. But others claimed that Ernest pestered her for it when she said she would keep it for herself. Ernest would carry the Civil War relic with him all his life.

He blamed his mother for destroying Clarence's spirit and his will to live. But the real reason for Clarence's suicide lay deeper than that, in the makeup of his genetic code. He had been on a frantic roller coaster ride all his life. His moods were subject to wild emotional swings punctuated by morbid bouts of depression. That combined with creeping paranoia, insomnia, and finally heart disease and diabetes had been at the root of his mental collapse.

Ernest was more like his father in that regard than he cared to admit. He was all too aware of his own broad mood swings, his own flights into euphoria and plunges into the depths of depression.

Clarence's death kept Ernest and Pauline in the states longer than they had planned while Ernest and Marcelline tidied up the family's financial affairs. Grace was afraid that she would not be able to pay her bills since Clarence had died virtually insolvent. Ernest had money coming in now and told her he would send her a monthly check for as long as she needed it, a promise he made good on.

Back in Key West, Ernest and Pauline made plans to leave once again. They left some belongings behind in case they ever decided to return to the tropical paradise. Finally, on April 5, 1929, Ernest and his family set sail for Paris.

Chapter Thirteen

Ernest's old buddy from the Toronto *Daily Star* reentered his life shortly after Ernest returned to Paris. Morley Callaghan was a novice reporter for the paper when he first met Ernest, the newspaper's European correspondent, a few years earlier. Morley was four years younger than Ernest. He stood five feet eight inches tall and had dark brown curly hair and blue eyes. He was lean and muscular and was known to be good with his fists, an accomplished boxer. He was in awe of Ernest from the moment he first saw him. Ernest was over six feet tall and broad-shouldered. He had a natural charisma that commanded everyone's attention when he entered a room.

"He made men want to talk about him," Morley wrote. "He couldn't walk down the street and stub his toe without having a newspaperman who happened to be walking with him magnify the little accident into a near fatality."

Ernest was high-colored and sported a heavy black mustache. He wore a peaked cap over his long black hair that "made him look like an Italian," according to Alice B. Toklas. His tweed jacket was baggy, bulging at the side pockets with notebooks and pens. Ernest looked every inch the writer and Morley hero-worshiped Ernest from the beginning and knew the older writer was destined for great things. Morley wanted to be just like him.

Ernest was happy to be his mentor even then, before Ernest had published more than a handful of stories of his own. He was eager to play the role of the older writer taking a younger man under his wing. With his star status at the newspaper, Ernest could afford to be generous.

"James Joyce is the greatest writer in the world," Ernest offered sagely. He said he wanted to read something Morley had written to see if it was any good. "I just wanted to see if you were another goddamned phony," said Ernest. "You're a real writer. You write big-time stuff. All you have to do is keep on writing."

These comments were gems from on high coming from the one man in the world whom Morley admired the most. Ernest had given Morley the true, true gen on what it took to be a world-class writer. "Even if your father is dying and you are there by his side and heartbroken," Ernest had said to Morley, "you have to be noting every little thing going on, no matter how much it hurts."

There it was then: never stop taking notes, not even at your father's funeral, not even when you are divorcing your wife and marrying her best friend. Take notes. Get it all down right so that you can write the truest sentences about it possible. Just start with the truest sentence you know and the rest will follow.

* * *

Morley arrived in Paris with his wife Loretto after quitting his newspaper job. His first novel, *Strange Fugitive*, had just been published, but sales were mediocre. He wanted to hook up with Ernest and Scott and become a part of the clique of expat writers and artists who had chosen Paris as their home away from home. Morley made the obligatory stop at Shakespeare and Company to meet the doyenne of expat booksellers, Sylvia Beach.

"At the desk sat a woman whom I knew, from pictures I had seen, to be Miss Beach," Morley wrote. "She was a fair, handsome woman in a severe suit, in her forties, I would have said; an Englishwoman; and in her manner there was something a bit severe and mannish. Yet she was an American. Having published *Ulysses*, she had become a famous woman. Writers in Paris, at least those who wrote in English, came often to her door. Her shop was a shrine for the Joyce lovers."

Morley had come to worship at the shrine.

He told Sylvia that he wanted to look up Ernest, so Sylvia wrote down Morley's address instead of giving him Ernest's and told him she would pass it along to the great man. Disgruntled at what he interpreted to be a brush-off, Morley grabbed his wife by the elbow and left the bookstore in a snit.

He and Loretto were sitting in their hotel room a few days later, eating croissants and drinking coffee after a late night of partying, when someone knocked on their door. Morley opened it and found the big novelist himself standing there in the corridor, a horseshoe-shaped scar stamped on his forehead and his six-year-old son Bumby by his side. Ernest took one look at Morley in his dark brown velvet bathrobe and shook his head from side to side.

"I haven't seen such a dressing gown on a man since the last time I saw Georges Carpentier climb into the ring," Ernest said to Loretto.

Morley laughed. This was a typical way for Ernest to break the ice and ease the tension after a few years of separation. Observe with the eye of a master novelist, instantly zero in on a singular characteristic, and deliver a semi-humorous, semi-barbed shot at point-blank range.

"What happened to your head?" Morley asked.

Ernest told him the story about the skylight falling on his head, an anecdote that has been embellished by numerous Hemingway biographers over the years. Ernest invited Morley and Loretto to accompany him as he took Bumby back to Hadley's place and then have a drink with him afterward. Ernest was now in a position to assume the role of the new Ford Madox Ford or Sherwood Anderson, bestowing his grace and wisdom on a fresh-faced young acolyte, which Morley craved. Morley didn't know it yet, but any paternal benevolence that Ernest showered on him was rooted in the knowledge that Morley would never write a better novel than Ernest had.

Ernest talked mostly about boxing on their slow walk along the rue Vaugirard, which put Morley instantly on his guard. Morley had done quite a bit of boxing in college, and Ernest appeared to be testing Morley's knowledge of the sport while simultaneously taking his measure.

After dropping Bumby off with Hadley, Ernest took them over to a café he knew on the Boulevard Saint-Michel where they could sit outside and see the river and the Cathedral Notre Dame on the Isle de la Cite. Ernest ordered beers for the three of them and then said, almost offhandedly, as if to establish a bond between himself and Morley and Loretto, who were devout Catholics, "I'm a Catholic now."

Morley had heard that Ernest's second wife was Catholic, and he assumed Ernest had converted to please her. Morley let the comment hang in the air between them, not sure where Ernest was going with it. But Loretto was curious.

"How were you able to get a divorce and marry within the Church?" she asked.

"It wasn't difficult," Ernest replied, "since Hadley had never been baptized."

How convenient that was. And how typical. In the eyes of the one, true, holy, catholic, and apostolic Church, Ernest's first marriage never existed and Bumby was technically a bastard.

Ernest may have converted to Catholicism, but at his core he was primarily a sensualist and would remain so all his life. "You only needed to look at his face, his eyes and his mouth," Morley wrote, "to know that he delighted in all that was sensuous. He had to savor all the sensations, know all the delights of the senses—with death apparently in his imagination like a presiding officer always asking him how he would take it when he came to the end of his knowing."

Ernest invited Morley and Loretto to visit him at his house and meet Pauline and Patrick. But not before he quickly downed seven beers to Morley's three during the course of the afternoon. After Ernest left, Morley turned to Loretto and asked, "Well, how do you like him?"

"Very much," she answered. "You can't help liking him. Tell me, has he changed at all?"

"No, he hasn't changed at all—except for one thing."

"What's that?"

"Didn't you notice about the beer and how he made it plain I couldn't keep up with him? Now he just has to be the champ."

Ernest liked Loretto too. But there was no indication that he ever had a wet dream about her all the time he knew her.

Chapter Fourteen

Morley and Loretto arrived at Ernest's spacious apartment at 6 rue Ferou. Morley remarked on a painting of a fish by Miro hanging on a wall—a different one than Ernest had given Hadley for her birthday shortly before he left her for Pauline—and another by Goya that Ernest had smuggled out of Spain. Ernest boasted that he was a friend of Miro and had also met Goya. Already he had become a master name-dropper. Next to a window sat an antique table and an ornate chair from Spain with a wide, sculpted, curving back.

Pauline came from money. Her trust fund was larger than Hadley's and threw off about thirty-six hundred dollars a year in income in addition to her salary as a fashion writer for *Vogue*.

Ernest led Morley and Loretto into the nursery and said, "Well, if you're interested in babies, there he is…" Patrick lay plump and dark-haired in his crib, gurgling up at Loretto who played with him while the two writers looked on. Then Pauline entered the nursery and beckoned them back to the living room where a maid was laying out a tray with tea and sandwiches. Pauline was small and dark, much shorter than the tall, fair Hadley. She was not a beautiful woman, but striking and intense in appearance with steady eyes and a determined expression on her face. She noted Loretto's silk suit and coral skirt and assumed she had bought them in Paris. No, Loretto said, she had made them herself. Pauline studied her quizzically; she had been a fashion writer before she married Ernest and was struck by Loretto's expertise in duplicating a style that was the talk of Paris at the time. The look in Pauline's eyes said she was not totally convinced that Loretto was telling the truth.

It was apparent immediately that Pauline was a different kind of woman than Hadley was. Hadley, with her open, trusting, unassuming demeanor, was no match for someone as aggressive and competitive as Pauline.

"Have you done any boxing?" Ernest suddenly asked Morley out of the blue, knowing full well that Morley had done a fair amount of boxing in college.

"Yes, I've done quite a bit of boxing," Morley said.

"Just a minute." Ernest left the room and returned a few moments later with two pairs of boxing gloves. "Come on, let's see." Ernest handed Morley a set of gloves.

"Oh, come on," said Morley, refusing to take the bait.

Ernest continued to hold the gloves out to him. "Come on, put them on," he said, a smile on his face with little mirth behind it.

"Here in this room?" Morley asked.

"Just put them on. I want to see."

Morley was in shock. He looked around the living room at the tea service on the table a few feet away, the antique table, the expensive chair from Spain. He looked at Loretto who stared back wide-eyed at her husband.

"You can't box here," she said. Loretto turned to Pauline for support, but Pauline just stared at her husband with a bloodlust of her own in her eyes. Pauline was more interested in seeing Ernest in action than she was concerned about any damage to her furniture.

Morley had no way out of it now. He laced on his gloves while Ernest laced up his. So there they were, the five-foot-eight-inch Morley who had grown something of a paunch by this time, and the brawny six-foot-plus Ernest with their gloves raised high. They circled each other like two panthers in a pit looking for an opening. Ernest lunged first with a left, and Morley ducked. Then Ernest let fly with a right, which Morley blocked. Morley countered with a few jabs and Ernest jabbed back. Then Ernest smiled broadly and started to unlace his gloves, a genuine look of pleasure plastered on his face.

"I only wanted to see if you had done any boxing," Ernest said. "I can see you have."

Why didn't you take my word for it? Morley wanted to ask, but he was immediately disarmed by the boyish pleasure Ernest had taken in their brief skirmish. He decided to chalk it up to Ernest being Ernest, a boy-man who couldn't rein in his impetuous nature. They sat back down and laughed. Ernest told Morley he missed boxing since none of his friends in Paris knew how to do it. Why don't we go boxing at the American Club not too far away? Ernest suggested. It would be just for the sport of it, just for the exercise. So Morley, at his ease now, agreed to stop by the following afternoon to pick up Ernest and box with him at the American Club.

"What did you think of Pauline?" Morley asked Loretto after they left.

"Nobody's edging in on Ernest while she's around," said Loretto. "It's a very big thing for her to be Ernest's wife, you know."

"Come on now. For her Ernest became a Catholic. I wonder what Pauline would have said if we had lurched around and broken her furniture."

* * *

The two writers established a routine. In the mornings they worked on their books, and once a week or so in the late afternoon Morley called for Ernest and accompanied him to the American club for a brisk workout with the gloves. Ernest was making final revisions on the galleys of *A Farewell to Arms*, and Morley was laboring away on a book of short stories. Catherine Barkley, Ernest's heroine in the new book, was seven years older than Frederic Henry, the main character—approximately the same age difference that separated Ernest and Hadley.

Ernest carried a gym bag containing the boxing gloves and gym shoes, and Morley strode beside him in rope-soled espadrilles. They discussed writing on their way to the club. Morley mentioned that he enjoyed Irish novelist Liam O'Flaherty's *The Informer,* and Ernest agreed that it was a fine book, although he had reservations about O'Flaherty's *Mr. Gilhooley.* A writer always gets himself in trouble when he starts thinking on the page, Ernest said. It is a mistake to let the reader see that one of his characters is doing the author's thinking. Morley took Ernest's comment to heart and felt he still had a lot to learn from him.

At the American Club they went down a flight of stairs into a back room with a cement floor. There were parallel bars in a corner and mats on the floor. An adjoining room contained a billiard table with some people playing. Ernest and Morley stripped down and laced on their gloves, and it was at this point that Morley realized he was about to go mano-a-mano with a man who stood four or five inches taller than he did and outweighed him by thirty or forty pounds. Ernest had established a reputation as a skilled and savage fighter who pulled no punches and asked for no quarter. Ernest was himself the source of many of these stories, of course. He once told his and Morley's and Scott's editor, Max Perkins, that he had jumped into the ring after a boxing match and knocked out the French middleweight champion with one punch. He told the story because he knew Perkins would repeat it to everyone who entered his office. The fact that the story was probably bogus made no difference; creating myths about oneself for others to spread was all that mattered.

Morley suddenly became terrified when he looked across and saw Ernest looming a few feet away with his hands held high, his chin tucked down toward his shoulder, looking every inch like a professional who could go ten rounds with the best of them. "Try and make him miss, then slip away," Morley counseled himself. They took each other's measure for the first three minutes, then took a break. At the start of the second round Ernest rushed over and trapped Morley in a corner, raining blows down on him. Morley hunched up like a turtle in its shell, thinking only of self-defense.

"Look, Morley," Ernest said, "never crouch that low. It's impossible to punch from that angle."

Morley was mortified. He realized that he had been afraid to engage Ernest and was interested only in surviving Ernest's punishing blows without trying to land any of his own. He was boxing defensively, and you can't win a fight unless you go on the offensive. Morley reminded himself that he had boxed the past winter with an intercollegiate heavyweight champion who was just as big as Ernest, against whom Morley had given a good account of himself.

At that moment he saw Ernest more objectively. He realized that while Ernest looked like a classic boxer at first, he was really more of a puncher whose timing was slightly off. Morley could call on his skills to sucker Ernest in by carrying his left low, then beat him to the punch before Ernest could get his right cross in motion. Morley's confidence grew once he understood that his skills were actually superior to Ernest's. Ernest was not that hard to hit. He didn't seem to mind taking a punch in an effort to land one of his own. Ernest took Morley's jabs and counterpunches like a good sport, enjoying the competition now that Morley was taking the fight to him, complimenting Morley whenever he got a good lick in. When they were finished for the day, Ernest laughed loudly, his adrenalin flowing from the contact. He invited Morley out for a drink to talk about sports, writing, and anything else that crossed their minds.

They sat outside on the sidewalk at a small café talking about sports. Morley had come to Paris to hook up with Ernest and Scott and further his writing career, and he rediscovered a good friend as well. Ernest was impossible not to like when things were going well for him and you didn't run afoul of the ugly side of his nature. He was childlike at his best. His boyish enthusiasm was infectious. Morley truly enjoyed spending time with him and found him fun to be with.

Then Morley made a mistake. He asked Ernest if Scott was in town.

"Not that I know of," Ernest said, and it was as though a dark cloud passed over the sun blocking its radiance. Ernest became silent and withdrawn. Morley was startled by the instantaneous change in Ernest's mood. Morley tried to reconnect, talking about their days working for the same newspaper in Toronto, but Ernest was unresponsive. Morley was desperate to recapture the camaraderie of moments earlier, but nothing he said could pull Ernest back out from behind the storm cloud. Morley had heard stories about Ernest's unpredictable mood swings, and now he was witnessing one first-hand. Then Ernest came around as quickly as he had gone away.

"I like Loretto very much," he said. "She has a kind of savage candor, hasn't she?"

Morley assumed he was referring to Loretto's question about

getting married in the Church. Seeing an opening, Morley lied and said that he liked Pauline as well.

Then, in another abrupt change of direction, Ernest reached inside his gym bag and pulled out his proofs of *A Farewell to Arms*. "Would you like to glance at them?" he asked.

Morley felt honored. Ernest ordered another drink while Morley read the first two chapters. He was instantly struck at how much Ernest's writing had matured from his first novel. There was magic in the way the words came cleanly together. His description of the landscape was done with the eye of a painter.

"It's going to be a bigger book than *The Sun Also Rises*," Morley said, genuinely impressed.

Ernest laughed, happy with Morley's reaction. "*The Sun Also Rises* was the kind of book you write in six weeks," he said. "Always remember this. If you have a success, you have it for the wrong reasons. If you become popular it is always because of the worst aspects of your work. They always praise you for the worst aspects. It never fails."

Chapter Fifteen

Morley and Ernest got together to box at least once a week, and Morley was careful not to mention Scott since that first day after their workout at the American Club. As it turned out, Morley ran into Ford Madox Ford before he had a chance to meet Scott. Morley had met Ford a few years earlier in New York and had been less than impressed by the man, even though he realized that no one loved good contemporary writing more than Ford did. Perhaps it was Ford's appearance that turned Morley off. Ford was an easy man to feel sorry for at first. He was big and clumsy, portly with an unkempt walrus mustache and a speech impediment caused by a gas attack suffered in combat.

Ford had helped so many writers, including Ernest, who disdained him later on—sometimes for good reason. After Ford described Robert McAlmon in print as one of the worst writers he had met in Paris, McAlmon responded as might be expected. "He wheezed and talked in an adenoids-clogged voice," McAlmon said of Ford, "often in a secretive manner, so that I had difficulty understanding him, and did not necessarily believe him when I did. On one occasion Ford assured me that he was a genius."

Harold Loeb, whom Ernest satirized unmercifully as literary dabbler Robert Cohn in *The Sun Also Rises*, was no less vicious. "Ford moved ponderously, with his feet at right angles to each other," Loeb said. "His hair was white, his teeth imperfect. His head resembled Humpty-Dumpty's except for the walrus mustache and the rosy complexion of a retired officer of the Indian army. He spoke with a slight, sibilant hesitation, as if he suffered from asthma. I was not favorably impressed." But Loeb allowed that Ford had some redeeming qualities.

"Yet after he sat down and we had talked a while, I felt drawn to him. Something of his spirit, courage, and generosity came through."

Morley, too, was disillusioned at first by Ford's carefully developed persona as "a literary man" who led "the literary life." But Morley could see that Ford was easily underrated. During a party at Ford's flat in Paris, Morley observed that while Ford played the buffoon, "those pale eyes of his were always on someone." And Ford was a master at plunging a barbed observation into someone's hide when it suited him, which he did into Morley's at a café after the party. Morley had incited Ford's wrath during one of Ford's self-indulgent parlor games, and Ford ridiculed him in front of his other guests with one of his penetrating digs.

Morley advised Ernest that Ford was not such a fool as he appeared to be. "Being gassed in the war gave Ford a great advantage," he told Ernest. "We have to lean forward attentively when he whispers."

"Gassed in the war?" Ernest shot back, refusing to give his erstwhile benefactor an inch. "Don't let him kid you. He was never gassed in the war."

Ernest was perhaps being a trifle defensive, considering that he appeared to be inflating his own wartime experience in his character Frederic Henry, Ernest's alter ego in the new novel. Then again, a lot of the blame rests with Ernest's readers and critics who tended to view the stories he told as literal interpretations of his own life rather than as fiction rooted in reality. Morley saw that distinction clearly.

"His imaginative work had such a literal touch," Morley wrote about Ernest, "that a whole generation came to believe he was only telling what he, himself, had seen happen, or what actually happened to him. His readers made him his own hero. As he grew older it must have had tragic disadvantages for him."

Boxing and writing were the common bonds that linked Ernest and Morley. And Morley's confidence in the ring with Ernest grew with each encounter. "In a small bar, or in an alley," said Morley, "where he could have cornered me in a rough-and-tumble brawl, he might have broken my back, he was so much bigger. But with gloves on and in a space big enough for me to move around, I could be confident."

When Morley returned home from one of his bouts, Loretto was horrified to see numerous black-and-blue marks across her husband's shoulders. Morley laughed and assured her that those marks meant that Ernest had missed his jaw and nose. After Morley slipped Ernest's punches one day and nailed him a few times on the mouth, Ernest said, "You're really a light heavyweight. It's the way you're built. I thought at first it was just fat on you."

Morley studied his own gut, knowing that his pot belly added an extra twenty-five pounds to his normal weight, and understood that Ernest was building his opponent up to level the playing field in his own mind. Still, Ernest took Morley's punches good-naturedly and complimented Morley on his boxing skills. The bartender at the Falstaff, an oak-paneled English pub off Montparnasse, asked Ernest what happened to his lip one day. Ernest laughed and said, "As long as Morley can keep cutting my mouth he'll always remain my good friend."

* * *

Robert McAlmon never would attain the financial success and critical acclaim that Ernest, Scott, and other writers of the era did, although he was highly regarded at the time by some of his contemporaries—Ford notably excluded. Robert's biggest problem was the reluctance of commercial publishers to publish his books, which dealt openly with homosexual themes. Ernest's story "Up in Michigan" was not the only one considered to be *inaccrochable*. Robert was married to a British writer named Annie Winifred Ellerman, who used the penname Bryher, but he was open about his bisexuality and his preference for slim young men. Stymied in his efforts to find a publisher, Robert started a magazine and then a book publisher, Contact Editions, primarily to publish his own work, and also early stories by Ernest, Gertrude, William Carlos Williams, and Bryher.

Morley and Loretto were strolling through the Left Bank one afternoon when they ran into Robert. "I'm having dinner with Jimmy Joyce and his wife at the Trianon," said Robert. "Why don't you join us?"

"I understand he hates being with strangers and won't talk about anybody's work," said Morley.

"Who told you all this?"

"Hemingway."

"Oh, nuts," Robert sneered. "Don't you want to see Jimmy? You'll like him. You'll like Nora, too."

Of course Morley wanted to meet Jimmy. Who didn't? It was like living in Rome and getting the opportunity to see the pope. Didn't Ernest say that Jimmy was the greatest writer in the world—even though a lot of what he wrote was even more incomprehensible than Gertrude's work? So Morley accepted and Robert told them to meet him at the Trianon in an hour and a half. The Trianon was located near the Gar Montparnasse and was notable for its good food and affordable prices. Robert was already there seated at a table to the right with Jimmy and Nora.

Morley recognized Jimmy from photographs of the novelist as soon as he walked in. Jimmy was dark, small-boned, and extremely thin with fine features. His eyeglasses were thick, almost opaque from an angle, and he was dressed in a dark suit. Nora was sensuous with her heavy breasts, and Morley could see instantly that she was Jimmy's inspiration for the long erotic Molly Bloom soliloquy at the end of *Ulysses*.

Ernest had misled Morley about Jimmy. Was it deliberate? Jimmy welcomed his guests with a chatty Irish charm, speaking with a soft and pleasant voice, punctuating every other sentence with a pun. Morley's father, a well-read man who loved poetry, had told him not long ago that Jimmy's prose was more accessible if you read it aloud with an Irish brogue. Now, listening to Jimmy in person for the first time, Morley understood exactly what his father meant. Jimmy's casual remarks were riddled with puns delivered in a soft Irish brogue that rendered his wordplay more comprehensible. His style of speaking, just as his style of writing, was unique. Morley suddenly felt a new respect for his father.

Robert excused himself as he stood up to go to the men's room. He was visibly drunk as he tottered away from the table—a frequent condition of his. When Robert was out of earshot, Jimmy leaned over and asked as calmly as he might inquire about the weather outside,

"What do you think of McAlmon's work?"

Stunned, Morley wasn't sure how to answer at first. He hesitated, then ventured, "McAlmon simply won't take time with his work. He's hypnotized himself into believing the main thing is to get the record down."

"He has a talent," Jimmy said softly, no trace of malice in his voice. Morley thought him incapable of malice. "A real talent. But it is a disorganized talent."

So much for Ernest's comment that Jimmy didn't like to discuss other writers' work.

When Robert returned to the table, Morley could smell vomit on his breath. Others had told Morley that when Robert got so drunk he couldn't drink any more without passing out, he excused himself, went to the men's room, and stuck his fingers down his throat to make himself nauseous. That allowed him to keep on drinking longer into the night. Morley wished that Robert would leave to seek out more bibulous companionship, but no such luck. Morley wanted to spend more time with Jimmy without Robert in attendance, just the two couples together discussing other writers. Robert had a tendency to monopolize the conversation the drunker he got; he talked interminably about subjects no one else wanted to hear about. Morley wanted to know what Jimmy thought of Ernest, Scott, Ford, Gertrude, and all the other literary lights of Paris, but he couldn't get a word in edgewise with Robert there in his cups. Finally, as though reading Morley's mind, Jimmy turned to Nora and asked, "Have we still got that bottle of whiskey in the house, Nora?"

"Yes, we have."

"Perhaps Mr. and Mrs. Callaghan would like to drink it with us."

Morley was delighted and honored. Here was a chance to discuss literature with the great Jimmy himself in the novelist's own apartment no less. When they set foot inside Jimmy's and Nora's living room, Morley took in the surroundings in a long studied glance. The very look and feel of the place could not have been more conventional. Jimmy was perhaps the most exotic and original writer in English of the day, yet his dwelling place might have been that of a working-class Dublin pensioner. Morley should have gotten a clue from Jimmy's plain dark suit that made him look more like an accountant than an avant-garde fiction writer. The young acolyte learned an important lesson that evening: the more eccentric a writer's work is, the more conventional his personal lifestyle is likely to be.

Chapter Sixteen

Max Perkins had told Morley in New York not to wait for a formal invitation from Scott. "Don't write to Scott. Don't be formal. Just drop in on him," the editor had said. Frustrated by Ernest's refusal to introduce him to Scott, Morley got his address from Max. Morley and Loretto sauntered over to the old stone building near St. Sulpice Cathedral where Scott and Zelda lived. As they approached the address, Morley said to Loretto,

"Why, this isn't more than a stone's throw from Hemingway's place."

As they searched the nameplates in the vestibule for Scott's name, a taxi pulled up in the street outside. Scott got out first and held the door for Zelda. Scott was slender, fine-featured, and handsome. The streetlight shone on Zelda's blonde hair and accentuated her alluring features. Scott was startled when he entered the vestibule and saw the two strangers standing near the doorbells.

"I'm Morley Callaghan and this is Loretto."

Scott hesitated a moment and then said, "Well, hello, how are you? Why didn't you let us know you were in Paris?"

Why not indeed? Goddamned Ernest!

Morley studied Scott and Zelda more closely as he and Loretto followed them upstairs. Scott was about the same height as Morley, well-dressed, and he carried himself with a studied dignity. Zelda was more handsome than beautiful and had a stubborn firmness in the set of her jaw and the look in her eyes. Their apartment was large and elegant, far more elaborate in appearance than any of the other apartments Morley had seen so far. Scott made them all drinks, and before Morley could ask him about his own work, Scott started to talk effusively about Ernest's new novel.

He showed Morley a manuscript copy of *A Farewell to Arms* and asked Morley if he had read any of it.

"Some parts of it," Morley said.

"Just listen to this," Scott said. He proceeded to read a passage that he liked in particular and asked when he was finished, "Isn't it beautiful?"

Morley was taken aback. Here was Scott, who had been first out of the gate with a world-class novel of his own, gushing like a schoolgirl over Ernest's yet-to-be-published novel in progress. Morley had indeed been impressed by the first two chapters Ernest had showed him, but in an effort to play devil's advocate, he qualified his response,

"Of course it's beautiful," Morley said, "but maybe it's too deliberate. Maybe the rhythmic flow is too determined, and the passage emerges as a set piece."

"All right, it doesn't impress you," said Scott, shrugging.

Before Morley could reply, Zelda blurted out, "If you ask me, it sounds pretty damned biblical!"

Zelda had been quiet until now, observing her guests intensely with her drilling eyes, but suddenly she grew talkative and started to babble about writing in general, dominating the conversation. Scott just stared at her, letting her drone on. He studied her as one might a caged animal who was exhibiting strange behavior. Then he cut her off in mid-sentence.

"You're tired," Scott said firmly. "You should go to bed."

Zelda deflated in front of all of them. She had ballet lessons in the morning, she apologized. She had to get up early. Without further word, she got up and disappeared into the bedroom. Morley and Loretto sat there stunned. As soon as Zelda left the room, Scott rose from his chair and poured himself another stiff drink. His face grew pale and his entire demeanor changed. He looked like a man who had just been poisoned and chose to ignore it. After a while he said,

"Let's have lunch tomorrow, Morley."

"I'd be glad to have lunch."

"Whom would you like to have lunch with us?" Scott asked. His pallor was ghastly.

"It doesn't matter, Scott."

"Clive Bell, the art critic, is in town. Do you know his work?"

"I've read his book," said Morley.

"No, I don't think he impresses you enough." Scott appeared to be on the verge of collapse.

"I'd like to meet him, if you'd like to have him along." Morley squirmed uncomfortably in his chair.

"No, I don't think Clive Bell impresses you, Morley. Who does impress you?"

Morley's face turned red with embarrassment. Loretto stiffened beside him. Scott rose slowly from his chair.

"Would this impress you, Morley?" he asked.

Scott got down on his knees, tipped forward onto his head, and tried to do a handstand. One leg went up in the air and then another before he belly-flopped forward. Scott laid there immobile, his face planted onto the rug. Morley jumped out of his chair and helped Scott to his feet.

"You're a little drunk," he said.

"No, not at all," said Scott, regaining his balance and assuming an air of dignity as though nothing out of the ordinary had taken place. He shook hands with Morley and Loretto and escorted them to the door.

"It was nice meeting you," said Morley.

Scott nodded goodbye and closed the door behind them.

Outside on the street, Morley shook his head in wonder and said, "He was drunk, that's all. Yet how did it happen to him so quickly?"

"Do you know you have the craziest friends?" Loretto said.

"Aren't you lucky? I'm the only one who is calm, objective, and rational."

* * *

The next day Morley wrote Scott and Zelda a note, thanking them for their hospitality and apologizing for barging in on them the way they did without calling first. Morley told Ernest about his bizarre meeting with the Fitzgeralds, and Ernest just shrugged and said, "Well, that's

Scott."

Morley found Ernest's reaction infuriating. Wasn't he supposed to be a friend of Scott? Why wasn't he concerned? Scott clearly needed help. The following day Morley and Loretto wandered around the neighborhood after lunch trying to make sense of the situation. When they opened the door to their flat, they saw three blue special delivery letters inside on the floor. The letters were from Scott, saying he was desperately trying to reach them. At that moment, their plump, red-haired Russian landlady knocked on the door and announced, "Your friends…"

Scott and Zelda were half a step behind her looking agitated. They both appeared to be upset. "Morley, I got your note," Scott said without preamble. "This is terrible. All afternoon we've looked for you."

Morley and Loretto were baffled. What might they expect now? What had propelled Scott and Zelda to search for them so frantically? Morley tried to reassure them that what happened the other night was unimportant. They all had too much to drink. But Scott refused to be mollified, and Zelda stared at Morley and Loretto with penetrating, unblinking eyes that Morley found unnerving.

"You see, Morley," Scott said, "there are too few of us."

Morley didn't know what to make of that remark. Too few of whom? Writers? Talented writers? Morley let the comment hang in the air between them. Where did Scott and Zelda intend to go with this conversation? Out of courtesy, Loretto asked them to sit down and make themselves comfortable. They couldn't sit down, they said. They were on their way to dinner. Did Morley and Loretto want to have dinner with them at the Trianon tomorrow night? Scott had arranged to sit at Jimmy's table since the great novelist was out of town. What else could Morley and Loretto do but accept?

They arrived at the Trianon, only to find Scott and Zelda sitting at a different table on the other side of the restaurant. This was *not* the table where Morley and Loretto had dined with Jimmy, Nora, and Robert a few nights earlier. Morley said nothing about it and walked to the left, not to the right, to join Scott and Zelda. Scott was obviously infatuated with the aristocracy of literary talent and wanted to be part of it, even while he didn't get it exactly right. As soon as Morley and Loretto sat down, Zelda blurted out,

"I write prose. It's good prose."

"I'm sure it is," Morley said, not so sure at all.

How else could one respond to that? Was Zelda trying to let them know that Scott was not the only one in the family with literary talent and that she was part of the aristocracy as well?

"Hemingway has charming manners, don't you think?" Zelda said. "He has the most charming manners of anyone I know."

"What do you make of Pauline?" Scott asked. "Do you find her attractive? Can you see her appeal for Ernest?"

This was uncomfortable territory, discussing Ernest's wife with a man who supposedly knew Ernest better than Morley did. "Pauline seems to be a very nice woman," Morley said innocuously.

"I have a theory that Ernest needs a new woman for each big book," Scott said. He had a conspiratorial tone in his voice. "There was one for the stories and *The Sun Also Rises*. Now there's Pauline. *A Farewell to Arms* is a big book. If there's another big book I think we'll find Ernest has another wife."

How prescient that insight would turn out to be! Ernest ended up with four wives by the time he killed himself. Was it possible that Scott had a better handle on Ernest than Ernest had on Scott?

The waiter took their orders and the two couples relaxed after a few glasses of wine and some *hors d'oeuvres*. Dinner passed pleasantly enough with both couples laughing and enjoying one another's company. The earlier tension dissipated in the glow of good food and drink and stimulating conversation. Afterward, they strolled along the boulevard aimlessly and continued their dinnertime conversation about books and writing. At that moment a switch seemed to go on inside Zelda's brain.

"What'll we do?" she asked, her mouth curved in a mad smile. "Let's do something. I know, let's go roller skating."

"Where do you go roller skating around here?" Morley asked. Roller skating was about the last thing he wanted to do just then.

"We can find a place," Zelda chirped. "Don't you want to go

roller skating, Loretto?"

"I'll go. I'm game." Loretto wanted to go roller skating about as badly as her husband did.

Morley observed Scott studying his wife with the same intensity he did in their apartment the first night they all met. It seemed to be a pattern: casual conversation followed by Zelda going nutty just before Scott fell off his own rocking chair. Scott reached out without warning and grabbed Zelda by the wrist.

"I'm putting you into a taxi now," he said firmly. "You go home now and go to bed."

A feeling of déjà vu swept over Morley and Loretto. Isn't this where they came in? And just when things had taken a turn toward normal. Zelda caved in before their eyes just as she had done that first night and meekly agreed to go home and go to bed. Scott flagged down a taxi and held the door for her as she climbed inside. She said goodnight just as the taxi whisked her off into the night.

"Zelda has to get up early in the morning," Scott said brusquely. "She's taking those ballet lessons."

He suggested that they stop at the Dome for an after-dinner drink, but no sooner did they go inside than he started to complain about the tourists who had taken all the good seats on the terrace. The tourist crowd was particularly heavy this year, Scott said with some bitterness, because they had read about the Dome and other Left Bank hangouts in *The Sun Also Rises*. He was half annoyed about the situation, and half envious because his own fiction failed to attract the same cult following. The tourists at the Dome brought Ernest back into the picture.

"Couldn't we all have dinner together?" Scott asked Morley. "Couldn't we get the Hemingways? Couldn't you suggest it to Ernest, Morley?"

Why don't you suggest it yourself? Morley wanted to ask. Weren't Scott and Ernest supposed to be good friends? What was going on between the two of them anyway? Ernest refused to introduce Morley to Scott, and now Scott was asking Morley—the new kid on the block—if he could set up a dinner date with Ernest and Pauline. Ernest didn't appear to give a damn, but Scott was revealing himself to be one of the most insecure men Morley had ever met.

"I will certainly suggest it," Morley said.

Chapter Seventeen

The following afternoon when Morley called for Ernest to go boxing, Ernest brought a stranger along with him, the painter Joan Miro. They made a comical trio as they walked along the boulevard: Ernest tall and burly, Morley four or five inches shorter, and Miro eight inches shorter than Morley at barely five feet tall. To complete the image, Miro was dressed in a dark business suit and a black bowler hat. His shirt was stiffly starched and had broad stripes running crosswise. Ernest and Morley were dressed as they should be, like two men going to the gym for a workout.

Ernest's Spanish was pretty serviceable by now, which was fortunate since Miro didn't know a word of English and Morley had no Spanish. Ernest had recognized the artist's talent early on and had been cultivating his friendship. His efforts paid off as Miro was just beginning to establish a major international reputation, which would drive the price of Ernest's paintings skyward. Miro beamed proudly as he quick-stepped along the sidewalk to keep up with the taller men. He was happy to go to the gym and be their timekeeper, Ernest explained to Morley.

Before they got to the American Club, Morley told Ernest that he had been out with Scott who suggested that they all have dinner together. Ernest immediately became wary and defensive. "You didn't tell Scott where I lived, did you?" he snapped.

"No, I didn't."

"If you're going to be seeing a lot of Scott, don't tell him where we live, eh?"

"Why not? What's the matter?"

"The Fitzgeralds will come walking in on us at all hours."

"Can't you tell them there's a baby in the house? Tell them Pauline has to get some sleep."

"It won't stop them." Ernest shrugged his broad shoulders. "And besides. Zelda is crazy."

"OK," Morley said.

When they got to the gym Miro took off his coat, folded it neatly, and made a serious show of pulling out his stopwatch to accurately count out the minutes. He became totally immersed in the match, playing his role conscientiously as though he were officiating at a bullfight in Spain. Ernest and Morley picked up on Miro's dedication to his task and got down to business like two professional fighters determined to give their best performances. Usually they laughed and joked with each other as they went through their paces. It was a brisk workout for both writers and they were sweating heavily when the session was over. Miro bowed toward both of them without breaking a smile. To him it had been no joking matter officiating at a contest between two manly gladiators.

Afterward they strolled back along the boulevard toward the Select, where Morley was meeting Loretto. Ernest knew that Loretto would enjoy meeting the painter, so he offered to accompany Morley and introduce her to Miro. They spent a few minutes exchanging pleasantries, then Ernest and Miro continued on their way. The tiny Miro insisted on carrying Ernest's gym bag with the boxing gloves. He said that it would be an honor for him. Morley and Loretto watched the odd spectacle of the writer and the painter receding into the distance, Ernest big and bulky and the impeccably dressed, birdlike Miro trotting beside him carrying the larger man's bag.

Morley told Loretto that it was unlikely that Ernest would agree to meet Scott and Zelda for dinner.

"There's something about all this that doesn't make sense," said Loretto.

"What doesn't make sense?"

"Ernest doesn't see Scott because Scott is a drunk, right?"

"And would upset his life and work. That's right."

"But look, Morley. What about that manuscript copy of *A Farewell to Arms* Scott showed us? Where would Scott get it?"

"Probably from Ernest."

"Exactly!" Loretto said. "You don't go around handing out

manuscripts to people you want to hide from, do you?"

Loretto's comment was incisive. Ernest rarely said anything positive about Scott's work, but Scott fawned like a schoolgirl over Ernest's writing. Ernest would never have been able to leave Boni and Liveright and sign with Scribner's if Scott hadn't introduced him to Max Perkins. Ernest was beholden to Scott as he had been to Sherwood Anderson and Ford Madox Ford before Scott. Ernest had needed Scott in ways he would not admit, but pretty soon he wouldn't need any of them any longer. There were layers upon layers of complexity in all of Ernest's relationships. Nothing could be taken on face value. Loretto was reasonably convinced that they would be seeing a lot more of Ernest and Scott—together—than Morley envisioned at the moment.

* * *

Scott was perfectly tailored in an expensive suit, every strand of his hair in place, his blue eyes flecked with green as clear as the afternoon sky. He noticed a copy of *The Great Gatsby* on the table in Morley's living room. His eyes twinkled. He smiled, outwardly pleased. Sales of his novel had been respectable but had fallen short of Scott's expectations. They were not up there in best-seller land. Scott and Zelda had an expensive lifestyle, and Scott had been forced to write formulaic stories for magazines to flesh out his income.

"It was too short a book," Scott said. "Remember this, Morley. Never write a book under sixty thousand words."

It sounded like a reasonable defense, but it was totally erroneous, purely defensive. Scott chose to overlook countless novellas that had enjoyed buoyant sales. Later in his life Ernest achieved great commercial success with *The Old Man and the Sea*, which measured out to less than half the word count Scott mentioned. There was no simple formula for literary riches. Scott invited Morley and Loretto to have a drink with him at the Ritz.

"Let's go," Morley said, reaching for his coat.

Scott hesitated, staring at Morley critically, appraising him from head to foot. "Would you go over to the Ritz wearing those sandals?" he asked. He looked personally offended by Morley's footwear.

Loretto sized up the situation instantly. "Imagine, Scott. Morley didn't notice he still had his sandals on."

Morley looked at his wife, then at Scott. He decided to fall in line. "Wait, I'll put my shoes on."

Scott, who had stiffened for a moment, loosened up and smiled at Morley. He told them a story about the best-selling author Louis Bromfield. Louis and his wife lived in a posh chateau outside of Paris and had invited Scott and Zelda for dinner a few years earlier. When they arrived, the wealthy writer received them in his house slippers, which to Scott was a mark of disrespect toward his guests. Scott said that he found Louis's demeanor unforgiveable, and after an awkward evening at Louis's home, Scott refused to have anything to do with him. Years later, when Morley met Louis for the first time, he recounted Scott's story about the slippers. Louis's eyes brightened as though illuminated by the first light of dawn. His jaw dropped.

"I always wore slippers in my home when my guest was someone I felt close to," he told Morley. "I always wondered why Scott had turned against me."

At their table at the Ritz, Scott turned to Morley and said, "Do you know, Morley, you have written some of the finest stories in the English language."

Morley was stunned. Here he was just beginning to establish his reputation as a serious writer, hoping that some of Scott's and Ernest's growing reputations would rub off on him, and Scott was deferring to him as he had to Ernest. Morley thanked him for the compliment, and then Scott switched gears completely.

"Have you seen Gertrude Stein yet?" he asked.

"No, I haven't," Morley said. Where was he going with this conversation? Morley had little regard for Gertrude. Her abstract prose was nonsense, he believed. Gertrude was nothing more than a trickster. She had nothing whatever to say, but she was shrewd enough to know that and camouflage her banalities with calculated literary obscurity. No, if others wanted to pay homage to a woman who was nothing more than a fraud, that was their business. But Morley was not interested in being sucked into her web.

Scott abruptly turned the conversation around to himself. "Do you know what my own story is?" he asked. "I was always the poorest boy at a rich man's school. Yes, it was that way at prep schools, and at Princeton too. Do you know I'm a millionaire now?"

There was no good way to respond to that remark. Morley and Loretto remained silent. Then Scott admitted that he didn't really have a million dollars in his bank account, but anyone making more than fifty thousand dollars a year was considered to be a millionaire by everyone else. Was that true? Morley and Loretto didn't think so. If it were true, Scott was at best a penurious millionaire, forced to write eight stories a year for the *Saturday Evening Post* for four thousand dollars a story. But he and Zelda spent every penny of it. He was constantly scraping for more money to support their extravagant lifestyle. No, Morley did not think that millionaires lived that way, even if it gave Scott pleasure to believe he was a bona fide millionaire. Scott had been working on a new novel, *Tender Is the Night*, for some time now, but it was going very…very slowly. Ernest blamed Scott's lack of progress on Zelda; she would do anything she could to undermine him. But Morley wasn't quite so sure. Scott had been working hard lately. Morley believed that Scott's lack of progress was due to his own lack of confidence in himself.

When they went their separate ways after their drinks, Scott flagged down a taxi. He looked in his wallet and saw that there was not enough cash in it. "Wait a minute," he said. "I may not have enough money. Have you got any money, Morley?"

Morley searched through his own wallet and pulled out two hundred francs, worth eight dollars at the time. Morley handed it over to his millionaire friend, knowing that he would never see it again. He consoled himself with the belief that if their roles had been reversed, Scott would have given him the money without hesitation. Before Scott departed, Morley admired his hat and said, "That's the grandest hat I've seen in Paris, Scott."

"It's an Italian hat," said Scott. He yanked it off his head and handed it to Morley. "Take it. I want you to have it."

Morley tried to give it back. The hat was not a quid pro quo for the money Morley gave him. Morley merely admired it and thought it looked good on Scott. But Scott was adamant. Finally, Loretto stepped in.

"I simply won't have Morley take that lovely hat from you, Scott. Give it back to him, Morley."

Scott figured he could bulldoze Morley, but something about Loretto's tone of voice convinced him that he would be fighting a losing battle with her. He smiled at Loretto and put the hat back on his own head. The taxi sped him off into the night.

Chapter Eighteen

Morley met Scott a few days later for drinks at the Deux Magots, and Morley later wished that he had never taken Scott up on his invitation. What followed a few days later as a result of that meeting shaped Morley's relationship with both Scott and Ernest for the rest of his life. It was a pivotal event, one for which Morley would be remembered most, and it had nothing to do with anything remotely connected to literary achievement.

Scott asked Morley about his boxing matches with Ernest and seemed miffed that he had not been invited to come along to witness them. Scott started to talk about Ernest in a way that Morley found embarrassing. According to Scott, Ernest was the most fearless, courageous, adventurous man he had ever met. Ernest did this, and Ernest did that. Not only was he perhaps the greatest writer of modern times, he was a war hero, a hunter, a fisherman, and a world-class athlete. In the process of building up Ernest, Scott appeared to be simultaneously tearing himself down.

"You think I'm a fairy, don't you?" he suddenly asked Morley.

Morley stared at him in shock. "You're crazy, Scott," he said. Morley wished he had been more sympathetic to Scott's state of mind, but he was annoyed at the same time. How could Scott, with all his talent, hold himself in such contempt? How could he idolize Ernest, hero-worship a man he supposedly knew better than Morley did? Yes, Ernest was a great writer and a courageous adventurer. Morley, too, valued Ernest's friendship. But Ernest was a flawed human being like everyone else. He was hardly a demigod. Morley didn't believe in demigods.

"Did you know that Ernest once knocked out the middleweight champion of France?" Scott asked.

Morley had heard that story before and never believed it. He attributed it to one of Ernest's tall tales about himself, one he told to Max Perkins knowing that Max would tell it to everyone who entered his office.

"Do you really think Ernest is that good?" Morley asked.

"Ernest is probably not good enough to be the heavyweight champion. But I would say that he is about as good as Young Stribling." Scott was referring to a famous light heavyweight at the time.

Morley stared directly into Scott's eyes. "Look, Scott," he said, enunciating every word carefully. "Ernest is an amateur. I'm an amateur. All this talk is ridiculous. But we do have fun."

"Could I come along with you sometime?" Scott was determined to see for himself if Morley was telling the truth.

A few days later, about three o'clock in the afternoon, just as Morley was preparing to finish working and pick up Ernest, he heard a knock on his door. Ernest was standing there smiling broadly, bigger than life, with Scott at his side. Ernest was relaxed and joking while Scott looked like a kid with wonder in his eyes as he prepared to go to his first boxing match. Ernest told Morley that they had just finished lunch and thought they would come around for Morley a bit early rather than wait for him at Ernest's place. Morley put his day's output in order and got ready to leave.

Morley observed Scott carefully when they arrived at the American Club. Scott's eyes were opened wide as he took in the surroundings like a movie camera recording the scene for posterity. He looked at the cement floor with the mats. He checked out the adjoining room with men absorbed in a billiards game. Scott was dressed in a jacket and tie as usual, and Ernest and Morley had on their street clothes. Ernest and Morley stripped down to their shorts. Ernest walked over to Scott and instructed him in detail about how to count out the minutes, three minutes for each round with a minute in between for a rest period. Scott stared at the watch, nodded that he understood. He was in awe of the entire spectacle, men geared for combat, the smell of sweat in the air, soiled laundry, leather, ropes, barbells, the unmistakable stench of a locker room.

Scott squatted and pushed the button on the stopwatch. "Time!" he yelled.

Ernest and Morley closed in on each other. Morley noticed that Ernest became careless early in the round. He charged in quickly, his left too low. Perhaps Ernest was trying to impress Scott and make quick work of the bout. Morley caught him squarely on the mouth, drawing blood from his lip. Ernest did not take it well. In the past, both contenders had taken each other's best punches and laughed them off. But Ernest was not laughing now. Perhaps he was embarrassed in front of Scott. Perhaps he had been mortified by the stunned look on Scott's face.

Ernest ignored everything he knew about boxing and turned into a savage brawler. He charged Morley recklessly, swinging wildly, trying to nail him with a knockout punch. Morley backpedaled and counterpunched, trying to avoid Ernest's blows while scoring with his own. Ernest shrugged off Morley's jabs and hooks like a maddened bull, trading them off for a chance to flatten Morley with a single blow. The round went on and on endlessly. A few of the men walked in from the billiards room to check out the action. Morley felt more tired than usual and couldn't figure out why. Ernest too was tiring. The round was interminable. In an effort to end it now, Ernest rushed at Morley with murder in his eyes, but Morley beat him to the punch. He nailed Ernest cleanly on the jaw, spinning the bigger man around and sending him sprawling onto the floor on his back. Ernest wasn't laughing, as he normally did when Morley hit him a good one. There was fury in his eyes.

"Oh, my God!" Scott yelled, breaking the tension. "I let the round go on for four minutes!"

No wonder both men felt tired. Not even the professionals fought four-minute rounds. Three minutes were standard throughout the sport.

"Christ!" Ernest howled, pushing himself to his feet. He glared at Scott who cowed away from him. "If you want to see me getting the shit knocked out of me, just say so! Only don't say you made a mistake!"

Ernest took Scott's error personally, refusing to believe it wasn't deliberate. Morley sized up the situation immediately. Scott had been so mesmerized by the action he failed to check the stopwatch. Clearly it had been an oversight. But Ernest refused to believe it wasn't deliberate. He stomped off to the shower room to wash the blood off his face. Scott rushed over to Morley. Scott looked like a schoolboy who had gotten caught disobeying his teacher.

"Don't you see I got fascinated watching?" he said to Morley. Please believe me, he seemed to be saying. Please make things right with Ernest. "I forgot all about the watch. My God, he thinks I did it on purpose. Why would I do it on purpose?"

"You wouldn't," Morley consoled him. But he knew deep inside that Ernest would never forgive Scott for his oversight and would convince himself that Scott did it deliberately. Morley knew instantly that nothing would ever be the same again between Ernest and Scott, and he was fairly sure that things wouldn't be the same between Ernest and him from that day forward. Ernest was proud and egotistical. He had come to believe in his own mythology, the stories he told about himself and others told about him. No, things would not be the same after that. The last thing Morley wanted was for Ernest to be his enemy. Ernest's friendship meant too much to him. But it would not be the same ever again.

"Ernest didn't mean it," Morley said to Scott, not believing his own words. "It's a thing I might have said myself. A guy gets sore and blurts out the first crazy thing that comes into his head."

Ernest appeared to be in better control of his emotions when he emerged from the shower room. A few minutes spent mopping the blood from his mouth had given him a chance to reflect and reevaluate what had happened. Ernest and Morley got back into it again, with Scott staring transfixed at the stopwatch as though his very life depended on keeping an accurate count for the next round. Ernest danced around, more cautious now, his dark and brutal side reined in. Both men sparred skillfully, punching, counterpunching, each man giving as good as he got.

"Time!" Scott called out precisely on the three-minute mark. As Ernest and Morley moved apart to rest between rounds, one of the billiards players sauntered over to Ernest. He was a slim young man wearing a vest, holding his cue by his side. "Excuse me," he said with a British accent. "I've been watching. Do you mind me saying something? Well, in boxing it isn't enough to be aggressive and always punching. If you don't mind me saying so, the real science of boxing is in defense, in not getting hit."

Ernest stood rock still and glowered at the young man. For one tense moment it appeared as though Ernest might uncork his deadliest wallop and send the youngster flying backwards into the billiards room. Ernest stared at him for a moment longer and then said calmly, "Do you think you could show me?"

"Well, I could try," the billiards player answered.

"Good. No, wait. Don't show me. Show him." Ernest pointed at Morley. "I'll watch."

Now Morley was pissed. This was between Ernest and the Englishman. Why did he have to drag Morley into it? Ernest told Scott to unlace his gloves and put them on the young man. Morley fumed while he waited, not knowing what he was up against. The slim young fellow looked unimpressive enough, but he could easily have been the United Kingdom's lightweight boxing champion. He and Morley squared off against each other, and it didn't take Morley more than a minute to realize that his opponent had no idea of what he was doing. Morley backed him into a corner and punched him at will as the young man cowered in fear.

"Stop!" Ernest called out, saving the interloper from a further drubbing. "I think I understand what you meant. Now show me."

Ernest, in effect, had used Morley as a guinea pig so he could size up the billiards player and see what he was made of. Ernest wasn't about to get knocked on his ass twice in the same day. Now that Ernest knew that the fellow had nothing to offer, it was his turn to have a go at him. The youngster was trembling like a leaf in a windstorm, wishing he had never opened his mouth. He tried to beg off, but Ernest would not let him off the hook. "No, come on. You've got to show me," Ernest insisted as he laced on Morley's gloves.

Ernest commanded the center of the boxing ring, his feet planted squarely as the young fellow put up his gloves and assumed a defensive position. Ernest extended his left arm and put his right fist on his hip, disdaining and mocking his opponent who wished he were anywhere but where he was at that moment. The Englishman covered up like a turtle in his shell, terrified that Ernest would soon be raining his deadliest bombs down on his head. But Ernest did nothing. He stood there, fist on his hip and the other outstretched, staring at the young man. After a long silent moment, the young man appeared to be on the verge of tears, thoroughly humiliated not only in front of Scott, Ernest, and Morley, but also in front of his chums observing him from the opening into the billiards room. He extended his gloves to Scott, begging him with his eyes to unlace them and let him get the hell out of there.

"I'm sorry," he said faintly. His voice was a mere whisper. "I really haven't done much boxing. I've read a lot about it. It looked much easier than it is." The young man did not make eye contact with his friends as he skulked back into the billiards room.

The three writers packed away the boxing gear and left the gym, not saying a word about what had transpired that afternoon. They discussed writing instead as they headed appropriately enough to the Falstaff, their favorite English pub, for a drink. Scott was noticeably subdued. Ernest was his usual buoyant self. Morley was a bit wary, wondering if their individual and collective relationships had been broken beyond repair. Morley hoped that word would not get around the Left Bank that he had knocked Ernest onto the floor that afternoon. That's not how he wanted to be remembered. He knew Ernest would never forgive him for it. But Morley knew as well as anyone that juicy gossip spreads like wildfire whether you want it to or not. There's simply no stopping it.

A few months later, Isabel Patterson drove the final nail into the coffin of Ernest's relationship with Morley. Writing in a November 1929 edition of the *New York Herald Tribune*, Isabel stated with utmost certainty that Ernest told Morley he knew nothing about boxing and challenged him to a fight. Morley, she said, proceeded to knock Ernest out cold in the first round. So there it was. No amount of protesting by either party could alter the perception of reality that Isabel had created. It was there in the newspaper for everyone to read. If it's in the newspaper, it must be true. Morley tried to set the record straight, to no avail. Ernest was convinced that Morley had planted the story. Or perhaps it was Scott. It didn't matter. The story, the legend, was carved in stone. That's how everyone would remember it.

Chapter Nineteen

A Farewell to Arms was published at the end of September 1929 and exploded out of the gate. Within a month the book sold thirty-three thousand copies. At the end of the year sales were up to fifty thousand, and on January 8, 1930, Max wrote to Ernest to tell him that sales were up over seventy thousand copies and climbing. The reviews were almost universally euphoric from the leading literary movers and shakers, including Malcolm Cowley, Clifton Fadiman, J.B. Priestley, Arnold Bennett, and countless others. A rave review by Dorothy Parker pushed Ernest over the top, from mere famous author to a legend in his own time.

Scott had been right; Ernest was not good enough to be the heavyweight champion of the world, but he had enough talent, luck, and determination to position himself as the heavyweight champion of American writers.

Paris had begun to lose its luster for Ernest and Pauline. Ernest had not forgotten Key West since his visit to the states. Quite the opposite; the funky key off the southern tip of Florida had been calling to him ever since he left. In the deepest recesses of his being he knew when he was there that he was not finished with Key West. He knew he would be returning, perhaps to make his home there.

Ernest and Pauline abandoned Paris early in 1930 and rented a place until their possessions caught up with them. Pauline was the one who first fell in love with a two-story, white stone house on Whitehead Street, which her uncle Gus bought for them for eight thousand dollars. The home was situated on a corner lot. It had a leaky roof and antiquated wiring, but it was one of the oldest buildings in Key West, solidly built with double porches and wrought iron railings around three sides. A tall iron fence and palm trees cordoned off the property from the street.

Ernest, Pauline, and Patrick were happy there for the next few years. They were happy until a young, sexy, blonde writer named Martha Gellhorn descended on Key West at the peak of Ernest's career. She caught his attention immediately.

Scott was right about that part of Ernest as well; he needed a new wife for every major book. Had Pauline been aware that wife number three would be visiting Key West a few years after she and Ernest set up housekeeping, she would never have agreed to leave Paris.

And *that* is the true, true gen.

Acknowledgements

The material for this book comes from several primary sources: *Hemingway* by Carlos Baker (Princeton University Press, 4th edition, 1972); *A Moveable Feast* by Ernest Hemingway (Scribner's, 1964); *That Summer in Paris* by Morley Callaghan (Macmillan of Canada, 1986); *The True Gen* by Denis Brian (Dell, 1988); *Hemingway: the Paris Years* by Michael Reynolds (W.W. Norton, 1999); *Hemingway: the Homecoming* by Michael Reynolds (W.W. Norton, 1999); *The Breaking Point* by Stephen Koch (Counterpoint, 2006); *Hemingway* by Kenneth Lynn (Harvard University Press, 1995); and *Hadley* by Gioia Diliberto (Ticknor & Fields, 1992).

About the Author

Jerome Tuccille is the author of more than twenty-five books, including best-selling, highly acclaimed biographies of Donald Trump, Rupert Murdoch, Alan Greenspan, and the Hunts of Texas, as well as several novels. Tuccille's last biography was the award-winning *Gallo Be Thy Name*, a history of the Gallo wine clan and its roots in organized crime. The author is vice president/communications at T. Rowe Price, a major financial services firm. He previously taught at the New School for Social Research in New York City and is a former third-party candidate for Governor of New York. He is a member of Authors Guild and American Society of Journalists and Authors.